Hannah's palms were cold and clammy, and she started to shiver uncontrollably. She quickly slammed the door shut and sat against it, breathing heavily. For a second, she felt as if turning her back to the noise and closing the door would keep whatever was out in the hallway from getting her.

That's ridiculous, Hannah thought. *There's nothing out there. I must have just imagined the noise. It was probably part of a dream.* She stood up and headed back to her bed.

Scratch, scratch, scratch.

POISON APPLE BOOKS

The Dead End by Mimi McCoy

This Totally Bites! by Ruth Ames

Miss Fortune by Brandi Dougherty

Now You See Me . . . by Jane B. Mason &
Sarah Hines Stephens

Midnight Howl by Clare Hutton

Her Evil Twin by Mimi McCoy

Curiosity Killed the Cat

by Sierra Harimann

SCHOLASTIC INC.

New York   Toronto   London   Auckland
Sydney   Mexico City   New Delhi   Hong Kong

For Jordan and Norman

ISBN 978-0-545-45986-0

12 11 10 9 8 7 6 5 4 3 2 1   12 13 14 15 16 17/0

Printed in the U.S.A.   40
This edition first printing, September 2012

Chapter One

It was Hannah Malloy's least favorite kind of day — the sky was cloudy and gray but it hadn't started to rain yet. The air in her bedroom was hot and thick. She'd been packing boxes for half an hour, and her tank top was already completely soaked with sweat. It was the beginning of October, but Tarrytown was in the middle of an unseasonable heat wave.

Figures, Hannah thought. *It's just my bad luck that it's a million degrees on moving day.*

Hannah picked up a framed photo of what looked like a happy family. The image showed a man in a dark suit, a pretty woman wearing a cream-colored gown, and two twelve-year-old girls in matching ruffly lavender dresses. Hannah thought the girls couldn't have looked more different. One appeared confident and happy, her soft blond curls falling over the shoulders of the purple dress, which contrasted nicely with her tan skin. The other girl looked miserable, her red hair pulled back in a frizzy halo around her head, and the light-colored dress making her pale, freckled skin look almost ghostly.

Hannah sighed as she placed the picture in a box. The junior bridesmaid dress had been just one of a long string of decisions that others had made recently on Hannah's behalf, without asking her opinion. First, her dad had announced that he was getting remarried in July. Then her dad's fiancée, Allison, had chosen the "darling" lavender dress for Hannah to wear to the wedding. And to top it all off, Hannah's new stepsister was Madison Van Meter, one of the prettiest — and meanest — girls in their seventh grade class.

Hannah's mom poked her head into the room.

"How's it going, sweetie?" she asked. Her mom's hair was pulled back in a bandanna, and Hannah knew she had been busily packing boxes all morning. Hannah glanced around her room, which looked almost exactly the way it usually did, minus the two boxes she had filled with books and other knick-knacks from her bookshelf.

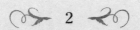

"Um, I'm almost done," Hannah lied. Her mom cocked her head and raised an eyebrow. It was obvious Hannah had barely packed a thing.

Hannah sighed. "I'm packing as fast as I can, Mom, I swear," she said.

"Well, your dad's going to be here in an hour and a half, so chop, chop!" her mom said brightly before she popped back out of Hannah's room and returned to her own boxes.

Hannah had thought things couldn't get worse than her dad marrying Madison Van Meter's mom — but then they did. A few weeks before, her mom had been offered a last-minute teaching job at the University of Chicago. Since Hannah's mom had been a student there, it was her dream job. The position was only as a midterm-leave replacement, though, and Hannah's mom didn't know how long it would last — it might be one semester, or it might be four. Since Hannah had already started seventh grade, her mom and dad agreed that it wouldn't be wise to pull her out of school and move her halfway across the country for an undetermined length of time. So they decided Hannah would move to the next town, Sleepy Hollow, where her dad had recently moved in with Allison and Madison.

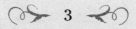

Hannah was happy for her mom, and she was glad she wouldn't have to change schools or move to Chicago. But that didn't mean she was excited about moving into the same house as Madison Van Meter.

Hannah's phone rang, and she snapped it up. It was her best friend and neighbor — for the next hour and a half, anyway — Paisley Lingren.

"Hey, Hannah Banana," Paisley chirped. Paisley was the only person in the world who could get away with calling Hannah that. "Are you still packing?"

"Yeah, I've still got a long ways to go," Hannah replied dejectedly. She knew she sounded pathetic.

"Well then, I'm coming over to help," Paisley said brightly. "Be there in a sec."

Less than three minutes later, Paisley appeared in Hannah's doorway. Her brown hair was tied back in a no-nonsense ponytail, and her sleeves were already rolled up. Literally. Hannah almost giggled. Paisley was the most efficient and organized person Hannah had ever met. And she had to be — Paisley was involved in so many hobbies and extracurricular activities it made Hannah's head spin. She never understood how Paisley managed to handle it all.

Hannah was much less organized and way less focused — up until recently, she had rarely stuck with any hobbies for more than a few months. But that had changed last year when her dad bought her a used guitar for her birthday. Hannah had immediately loved playing, and she looked forward to her weekly lesson more than almost anything.

"Hannah, this is a disaster!" Paisley scolded as she surveyed the messy room. "You've barely packed a thing!"

"I know, I'm a complete mess," Hannah admitted. "I need you, Pais. That's why you're my best friend."

"Okay, hand me a box," Paisley ordered. "I'll hold something up, and you tell me 'yes' or 'no.'"

Paisley headed to the closet and grabbed Hannah's favorite sneakers. Hannah gave her a thumbs-up. Then Paisley pointed to a pair of old ballet shoes.

"Um, no, obviously," Hannah replied. She hadn't taken ballet in years.

Paisley picked up Hannah's hiking boots. Hannah paused. Before the wedding, she had spent every Saturday with her dad. It was part of the custody arrangement after her parents had gotten divorced, when Hannah was four, and it was the one other thing besides guitar that she looked forward to each week. On their "special Saturdays," Hannah and her dad would bike, kayak, or go hiking in the summer, and snowshoe or snowboard together in the winter.

But since the wedding, Hannah's dad had barely had time for her, thanks to his two-week honeymoon in Hawaii and all of the renovations he had been helping with at Allison and Madison's house. Hannah knew more than she wanted to about how the master bedroom was being redecorated, and how her dad and Allison were turning the garage into a home office so her dad wouldn't have to drive to the university every day.

Hannah considered the boots. "Okay, yes," she finally told Paisley. Maybe her dad would have more time for hiking now that Hannah was going to be living with him.

She and Paisley managed to pack up most of her room in the next hour. Then Paisley's digital watch beeped.

"Aw, shoot," Paisley said. "Clarinet lesson in fifteen . . . I've gotta run. Sorry, Hannah."

"That's okay; I understand," Hannah said, giving her friend a quick hug. Hannah knew that being friends with Paisley meant putting up with her overpacked schedule. "You were a huge help."

"No problem," Paisley replied. "I'm gonna miss you, neighbor."

"I know," Hannah said sadly. "But we'll still hang out. See you in school on Monday?"

"Yup, see you then," Paisley said with a wave. She almost crashed into Hannah's mom on the way out of the room.

"Whoa, sorry, Ms. M.!" Paisley said. "Gotta dash — clarinet lesson in ten! Have fun in Chicago!"

With that, Paisley flew down the stairs and out the door.

Hannah's mom shook her head. "That girl certainly keeps herself busy. I don't know how she does it."

"Me neither," Hannah said with a laugh.

"Your dad's going to be here any minute," her mom said as she handed Hannah a large plastic pet crate. "Why don't we find Icky and get him into this thing?"

Icky was short for Ichabod Crane — the cat Hannah's parents had adopted when she was three. Hannah had been too little to pronounce "Ichabod," so she had shortened it to Icky, and that had been his name ever since.

Luckily, Icky was going to be moving to Sleepy Hollow with Hannah, which made her feel a little bit better about the move. She might be leaving the only home she'd ever known, but at least she wouldn't be doing it alone.

Hannah knelt down to peek under the bed, which was usually Icky's favorite hiding spot, but she didn't see him anywhere. Next she tried the closet, behind her desk, and finally, the laundry hamper. No Icky.

Hannah heard a car pull up in front of the house, followed by three short beeps. It was her dad's signal. She hurried downstairs with the empty carrier.

"Mom, I can't find him," Hannah called. "And Dad's already here." Hannah knew her father hated waiting.

Her mom emerged from the kitchen holding a bag of cat treats.

"Don't worry about your father. This time, he'll have to practice a little patience," she said. She shook the bag of treats. "Maybe this will tempt that cat. Icky, where are you, boy?"

Hannah and her mom canvassed the first floor of the house, but they couldn't find Icky anywhere. Hannah was sure she'd checked all his favorite hiding places. All except one.

"Behind the china cabinet!" she exclaimed. It had been Icky's favorite hideout when he was a scared little kitten. Sure enough, when Hannah peered behind the massive piece of furniture, she saw a black ball of fuzz with glowing yellow eyes and two white paws.

"Come on, Icky," Hannah said gently. "I've got a jerky treat just for you."

Just then, Hannah heard the creak of the screen door. She turned to see her dad stepping into the house, his arm still holding the front door open.

"What's taking so long, Hannah?" he asked.

Out of the corner of her eye, Hannah saw a streak of black emerge from behind the china cabinet, the white patch on Icky's tail flashing as he dashed straight out the open front door.

"Icky, no!" Hannah cried as she pushed past her dad and ran after the cat. She raced to the bottom of the driveway and surveyed the block desperately, but there was no sign of Icky anywhere.

In an instant, he had disappeared.

Chapter Two

Hannah ran back into the house, almost knocking her dad down a second time, tears stinging her eyes.

Mr. Malloy grabbed her arm as she flew past him.

"Hannah, slow down a minute!" he admonished her. "I'm sure he's just outside hiding under a shrub. I'll go look for him," he said, and slipped out the door.

Hannah sat down on the stairs with a thud, her shoulders hunched. In just a second, all of her nerves about the move had returned tenfold. Suddenly, Hannah wasn't sure how she was going to say good-bye to her mom without having Icky with her. Hannah's mom sat down next to her and put her arm around her, pulling her in for a hug.

"Oh, Mom!" Hannah burst out, tears running down her face. "This is the worst!" She knew she was being melodramatic, but she couldn't help it. Sure, Icky ran out into the yard every once in a while. Sometimes he even came back in a few minutes, but other times it took him hours. If he didn't get back soon, Hannah was going to have to leave without him. And suddenly, she just couldn't bear the thought of spending the night in a new house without Icky by her side.

"Hannah," her mom said soothingly. "He'll be back soon. You know Icky. He loves to dash out and roam the neighborhood for a bit, but he's always back by nightfall. He doesn't like to miss a meal."

Hannah knew her mom was probably right, but she couldn't help feeling that this time things were different. Icky's sudden disappearance was definitely *not* a good omen.

"Well, I'm not leaving until he comes home, then," Hannah said, crossing her arms decisively.

The screen door squeaked as Mr. Malloy came back inside, empty-handed. He shrugged apologetically at Hannah.

Hannah's mom stood up. "Well, my flight doesn't leave until tomorrow evening. I'm sure Icky will be back tonight, but it may not be for a while. So, Hannah, you go ahead with your dad, and I'll bring Icky over there tomorrow on my way to the airport."

"But, Mom —" Hannah tried to protest, but her mother held up her hand, cutting her off.

"There's no reason for you not to go with your dad now, Hannah," she said firmly. "That way you'll have the evening to settle in, and you can unpack all day tomorrow before school on Monday."

Hannah sighed. There was no use trying to argue when her mom had clearly made up her mind. Ms. Malloy was more stubborn than most parents.

Hannah and her dad loaded her boxes into the trunk and backseat of her dad's car. By the time they were finished, the sun was just starting to set, and there was still no sign of Icky.

Hannah climbed into the passenger seat reluctantly, keeping an eye out for Icky as she waved good-bye to her mom. Her dad patted her knee gently as he pulled the car out of the driveway, but Hannah turned away from him, crossing her arms across her chest and looking out the window. She knew her dad hadn't let Icky out on purpose, but she was still angry with him.

"I'm sorry about the cat, Hannah," he said, as though he was reading her mind. "I didn't mean to let him out. I'm sure he'll turn up, though. He always has before, right?"

Hannah could tell he was trying hard to smooth things over. It felt really weird to be mad at him. Since she saw him usually only once a week, Hannah hardly ever fought with her dad. Still, as much as she wanted to forgive him, she wasn't quite ready. She continued to stare sullenly out the window.

"Come on, Hannah," her dad pleaded. "Don't give me the silent treatment. I'm really looking forward to having you come live with Allison and me. Let's not start off on the wrong foot, okay?"

Hannah sighed. Unlike her mom, she wasn't particularly stubborn. It was pretty easy to wear her down. "Okay," she agreed reluctantly.

"That's the spirit!" her dad said. "I just know we're going to have such a great time together — you, me, Allison, and Madison. A real family."

A real family? Hannah thought. Isn't that what she and her mom had been? Her parents had gotten divorced so long ago that Hannah barely remembered a time when they'd all been together. Still, her dad's words stung unexpectedly. But he didn't even seem to notice he'd said something insensitive.

"And isn't it great that Madison is in the seventh

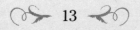

grade, too?" he continued cluelessly. "You can share clothes and have sleepovers every weekend, or whatever it is you girls do. And you'll even have someone to sit with on the bus!"

Hannah glanced over at her dad. Was he kidding? Had he *met* Madison? Clearly he could tell that Hannah and Madison weren't BFF, right? *Or not*, Hannah thought as she watched her dad fiddle with the radio, completely unaware that Hannah was still upset with him. A cheesy song from the 80s filled the car.

"Oh, I love this one!" her dad shouted before he started to sing along.

Hannah stared gloomily out the window again. Suddenly, she couldn't wait to get to her dad's place, where at least she could be alone in her room.

A few minutes later, there was a gravelly *crunch* as the car pulled into the driveway of a pretty Victorian-style house with a tiny front porch, complete with flower boxes and a swing. It looked like a scene out of a magazine. The only things that didn't quite go with the picturesque setting were the tombstones that bordered the property.

Hannah did a double take. *Wait, tombstones?* she thought, suddenly alarmed. Didn't terrible things happen to people who built houses on top of dead people? This was the first time Hannah was even seeing the house she'd be staying in for the next few months, and she couldn't believe her dad hadn't mentioned that it was practically sitting on a heap of ancient bones. Ever since he had moved in at the beginning of the summer, her dad had insisted on picking Hannah up whenever they spent time together. She had figured it was because the house was under construction, but maybe it had been because he was afraid she would freak out when she saw how close the house was to the graveyard.

"Um, Dad? You didn't tell me you live in a cemetery," Hannah said as she got out of the car. She had meant to sound annoyed, but instead her voice sounded shaky and scared.

"Ha-ha, kiddo," her dad replied. He walked to the back of the car and popped open the trunk, retrieving a stack of boxes. "You won't be living *in* the cemetery, just next to it. And it's not just any cemetery — it's the one made famous by Washington Irving's 'Legend of Sleepy Hollow.' How's that for a cool literary factoid?"

Hannah groaned inwardly. Sometimes it was incredibly annoying having two English professors for parents. Her dad in particular had a habit of constantly spouting what he called "cool literary factoids."

Hannah had grown up on tales of ghosts, witches, bats, and other creatures of the night that lived in the Sleepy Hollow Cemetery. Still, as far as she knew, none of her classmates had ever known anyone who had personally been haunted. The stories always began, "My friend's cousin Ely's friend Sam . . ." Logically, Hannah knew she wasn't going to encounter any ghosts or goblins. But still . . .

"I hope living next to the cemetery won't make you uncomfortable, Hannah," her dad said, as though he was reading her mind again. "I know kids in this town love to tell stories, but I think you're old enough to tell the difference between fact and fiction."

If there was one thing Hannah hated, it was an implication that she wasn't mature enough to handle something. So there was no way she was going to admit to her dad that even if she didn't believe in ghosts, there was still something creepy about living next to an old graveyard.

As she followed him into the house, Hannah wondered what other unpleasant surprises were in store for her that evening.

Chapter Three

Hannah's stepmom, Allison, greeted them at the door and made a big fuss as she grabbed the purple sleeping bag in Hannah's arms.

"I've got this!" Allison chirped as she headed up the stairs. "Follow me! I'll show you to your new digs."

Digs? Hannah rolled her eyes. Adults could be so ridiculous when they tried to sound young and cool.

When Hannah got to the top of the stairs, she saw that there were two doors in front of her — one door to the left and the other to the right. As Allison flung open the door on the right, a blast of hot air enveloped Hannah.

"Well, it's nothing fancy, but this is it," Allison said almost apologetically.

Hannah looked around. The sloping ceiling and walls were covered with posters and photos of basketball, baseball, hockey, and football players. The room obviously belonged to a boy.

Allison noticed Hannah silently taking in the sports paraphernalia.

"This is usually my son Greg's room, but he just left for college last month," she explained. "I'm sorry your dad and I haven't had a chance to take down all these posters and repaint the walls yet. We've just been so busy with the renovations downstairs. But feel free to do whatever you like — I'm sure Greg won't mind if you store his posters in the closet, as long as you don't tear them."

Right, Hannah thought. *The renovations.* It figured that in the three weeks since they'd all found out Hannah was going to be moving in, no one had even taken the time to take down a few posters in the room where she'd be staying.

"It's fine," Hannah said glumly. "It's really hot in here, though." She reached up and tugged on the cord hanging from the antique ceiling fan. Nothing happened.

"Oh, that's not going to work," Allison said. She crossed the room and pushed open one of the windows. "The ceiling fans in this house have been broken for years. I keep forgetting to ask the electrician to take a look at the wiring."

There was an awkward silence as Hannah tried to think of something to say. Thankfully, she heard her dad's footsteps coming up the stairs. A few seconds later, he appeared in the doorway.

Hannah grabbed a box out of his arms.

"Thanks, Dad," she said, relieved to no longer be alone in the stuffy room with Allison. "Why don't I come downstairs and help you bring in the rest of the boxes?"

Allison seemed relieved as well.

"Perfect," she said, a bit too brightly. "And I'll go check on the contractors. They should be about done for the day, and I want to make sure they've made some progress since I last checked in. Sometimes they just work so slowly!"

An hour later, Hannah was alone in her new room, unpacking her things. She had just finished arranging her shoes in the closet when she felt a sudden chill. Goose bumps swept up her arms, and the hairs on the back of her neck prickled. She was certain someone was watching her. Hannah whipped around. Sure enough, Madison stood in the doorway, arms crossed, with a nasty scowl on her face.

"Dinner's ready," she snapped at Hannah. Then she sauntered casually into the room. She picked up a black cat figurine Hannah had placed on the dresser. Madison turned it over in her hand and gave it a tiny toss into the air. Hannah gasped as Madison caught the figurine easily and let out a mean little laugh. She placed it back on the dresser, not very gently.

Madison took a step closer.

"Let's get a few things straight around here," she said menacingly. "See that door over there?" She gestured over her shoulder.

Hannah nodded.

"That's the door to *my* bathroom," Madison explained. "My mom said I have to let you use it, too." She rolled her eyes dramatically.

"But since the only way in is through this room or my bedroom, you'd better remember to unlock my door when you're done in there," Madison continued. "Because if you lock me out of my own bathroom, I will *not* be happy."

"Okay, fine," Hannah squeaked softly. "Can we go eat dinner now?"

"One more thing," Madison said. "If you ever touch even a drop of my shampoo, conditioner, body lotion, or anything else in there, you will be sorry. See you later, *sis*."

And with that, Madison turned and strode out of the room. *Talk about an evil stepsister!* Hannah thought. It was as if Madison had been taking lessons from Cinderella's tormentors.

Things didn't get much better at dinner. Allison served meat loaf with mushroom gravy and green bean casserole. Hannah didn't want to be rude, but there was nothing she hated more than mushrooms, and green beans weren't exactly her favorite, so she barely ate anything. And Madison spent half the dinner chattering on and on about her trip to the mall with her friends that afternoon. Then Allison and Hannah's dad spent the rest of the meal rehashing the plot of a movie they had seen the previous night. No one made any effort to include Hannah in either conversation, so she just sat there, silently swirling mushrooms around on her plate.

By the time dinner was over, Hannah was eager to just go to bed. She didn't think the day could get any worse, and the sooner she fell asleep, the sooner it would be over.

Even though it was only 8:30, Hannah pulled on her pajamas, grabbed her toothbrush, and headed for the bathroom. She jiggled the doorknob but it didn't budge, so she tried knocking. No answer. Hannah flopped down on her bed to wait. As soon as she did, her phone chimed. It was a text from Paisley.

wanna skype?

OMG! yes! logging on now.

Hannah quickly booted up her computer and opened the video chat program. She accepted the incoming call from Paisley, and her best friend's face filled the computer screen.

"Hey!" Paisley waved at her friend. "How's the new place?"

Hannah moved her head so Paisley could see the room behind her. "See for yourself."

"Um, nice posters," Paisley joked. "I didn't realize you were so into basketball. Are you going out for the team?"

"Ha-ha." Hannah stuck out her tongue at Paisley. "Today hasn't been the best day of my life, that's for sure."

"Oh no! What happened?" Paisley asked, her brow furrowed with concern.

"Well, first Icky ran out of the house while my mom and I were trying to get him into his crate."

Paisley gasped. "That is totally tragic! But you got him back, right?"

"I don't know," Hannah replied glumly. "Hopefully he's back at my mom's by now, but he was still missing when I left. He runs off every now and then, but he never stays out overnight. My mom's going to bring him here tomorrow on her way to the airport."

"I'm so sorry, Hannah." Paisley spread her arms out wide. "Virtual hug!"

"Thanks," Hannah replied softly. "Things didn't get much better after that. Madison's been, well, Madison. And you probably can't see out the window behind me, but you'll never guess what you can see from my bedroom."

Paisley shook her head. "You're right — I have no idea."

Hannah lowered her voice. "It's the Sleepy Hollow Cemetery!"

"Oh, that is *creepy*!" Paisley replied with a shudder. "You've heard the stories they tell about that place, right?"

Hannah nodded. "Yeah, but they're all pretty silly. And it's not like I actually know anyone who's ever been haunted, and I've lived around here my whole life."

"Well . . ." Paisley began hesitantly and then paused. "There is *one* story about a ghost cat. I don't want to freak you out, though."

Hannah had heard of the ghost cat before, but she couldn't remember the details. It was clear that Paisley knew the story and wanted to tell her, though. Paisley tended to believe in all of the Sleepy Hollow legends way more than Hannah did.

"No, it's okay," Hannah replied gamely. "You'd better tell me. I'd rather be prepared when a ghost shows up on the front porch."

"Okay, you asked for it," Paisley warned, but Hannah could tell her friend was thrilled to be playing the role of storyteller. "So the legend is that there was a little girl who lived in Sleepy Hollow in, like, the 1800s. She had this little black cat that followed her around everywhere. Then one day, she and the cat both disappeared. It was, like, poof, they were gone!

"They were missing for days, until some townspeople found the girl's dead body in the Hudson River. No one ever saw the cat again, though — well, at least not alive."

Paisley shuddered and lowered her voice dramatically. Even though Hannah wasn't even sure the story was true, she felt chills shoot up her spine. The wind outside rustled the leaves of the trees in the yard, and a cool breeze wafted through the window. Hannah glanced involuntarily over her shoulder at the window, but there was nothing there.

"You sure are good at telling ghost stories, Pais," Hannah said with a nervous laugh.

"And I'm not even done yet!" Paisley continued, her voice a hushed whisper. "The little girl was buried in the Sleepy Hollow Cemetery. Supposedly, the ghost of the cat still haunts the cemetery. Some of the townspeople think the cat had something to do with the little girl's drowning. And this is the craziest part — you know my aunt Suzie and my cousin Clark, who live in Stamford?"

Hannah nodded.

"Well, before I was born, they lived in Sleepy Hollow, probably pretty close to your dad's house. I know it was near the cemetery. Anyway, one day the basement of their house totally flooded — *and there hadn't even been a rainstorm!*"

Paisley paused dramatically again, and Hannah laughed.

"Maybe one of the pipes burst," Hannah suggested. "That happened in my mom's house a few years ago, and it definitely wasn't because of a ghost."

"Well, that's what they thought at first," Paisley said ominously. "But you'll never guess what they found floating in the water in the basement."

Hannah felt her heartbeat quicken. "What?" she squeaked.

Paisley's voice was deadly serious.

"A drowned black cat."

Chapter Four

After listening to Paisley's ghost story, Hannah had trouble falling asleep. She told herself it wasn't because of the scary story; it was because she was sleeping in a new house and had had a long, stressful day. But she couldn't seem to get the image of the dead cat floating in a pool of water out of her mind. For some reason, Hannah kept imagining Icky as the cat. Finally, after a lot of tossing and turning, she fell into a restless sleep.

Scratch, scratch, scratch.

Suddenly, Hannah sat up in bed. There had been a sound at her bedroom door. The room was pitch-black, and the clock on her bedside table read 2:44.

Scratch, scratch, scratch.

Hannah heard the sound again. It was definitely

coming from the door. *Of course!* Hannah thought. *It must be Icky, scratching to get in!* He often clawed at her door at night when he wanted to curl up on her bed.

Hannah jumped out of bed and crossed the room. She pulled the door open and gasped. The hallway was empty.

Suddenly, her surroundings came into focus, and memories of the previous day came flooding back to her. She was in her dad's house, not her mom's! The scratching at her bedroom door couldn't have been Icky, because he wasn't here. In her sleepy state, she'd thought she was in her old bedroom.

Hannah's palms were cold and clammy, and she started to shiver uncontrollably. She quickly slammed the door shut and sat against it, breathing heavily. For a second, she felt as if turning her back to the noise and closing the door would keep whatever was out in the hallway from getting her.

That's ridiculous, Hannah thought. *There's nothing out there. I must have just imagined the noise. It was probably part of a dream.* She stood up and headed back to her bed.

Scratch, scratch, scratch.

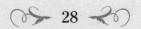

"Ahhh!" Hannah yelped. This time, the scratching sound had come from the window near her bed. Hannah rushed over and peered outside. Maybe it had been a tree branch scraping against the glass. Sure enough, the moon lit up a tree about seven feet from her window. But Hannah quickly realized that none of the branches came close enough to touch the window. In fact, the closest branch ended about three feet from the house.

It's got to be the other window! Hannah ran across the room to the window over the desk. But there weren't any trees anywhere near it.

Hannah wasn't sure what to do next. Should she go downstairs and wake her dad? What would she tell him? That she heard a scary noise and couldn't sleep? That seemed so babyish. After a few minutes, Hannah decided she would just have to go back to bed. Before she did, though, she dragged the desk chair over to the door to the hallway and lodged it firmly under the doorknob. *Better safe than sorry*, she thought as she climbed back under the covers.

She pulled the sheet up over her head the way she would have when she was a little kid. She used to believe that as long as one of the blankets covered her ears, no monsters could get her in the night. Hannah knew it was a silly little game invented by her five-year-old self, but she did it anyway, just in case. Finally, after a long time, she fell back to sleep.

Hannah spent the next morning unpacking the rest of her boxes and trying to put the weird scratching sound she had heard the night before out of her mind. It wasn't hard to stay shut up in her room for most of the day, since the rain that had been threatening the previous afternoon had finally started, and it was grim and damp outside.

By four o'clock, Hannah's mom still hadn't showed up. Finally, just before five, Hannah heard a car pull into the driveway.

She dashed downstairs and threw open the front door. Her mom stood on the porch empty-handed, her hair dripping. Hannah's face fell.

"Where's Icky?" she asked, her lower lip trembling.

"Oh, sweetie," her mom said softly. "He never came home last night. I waited until the last minute to come by today, but if I wait any longer I'll miss my flight. I was sure the rain would drive Icky home, but he just hasn't reappeared yet."

Hannah felt like she had been punched in the stomach. That morning had been the first in Hannah's life when Icky hadn't woken her up with his meows. And now all she had to look forward to this week were more mornings without him. He was gone — and worse, what if he never came back?

Hannah pushed the thought from her mind, but another alarming idea occurred to her instead. "What happens if he comes home tonight?" she asked desperately. "No one will be there to meet him!"

"The renters are moving in tomorrow, and I left them detailed instructions on what to do when he does come home," Hannah's mom explained. "There's extra cat food there for him, and they're supposed to call you right away so you and your dad can go over there to pick him up."

Hannah couldn't stop the tears that began to slip down her cheeks. She stifled a sob, and her mom pulled her in for a hug.

"I'm so sorry, Hannah," she whispered. "This certainly isn't the way I wanted to leave for Chicago. But I'm sure Icky will be home soon, and the Hendersons are a lovely family. They'll call you as soon as they see him. Plus, you can ask Paisley to keep an eye out for him as well."

Hannah's mom wiped Hannah's cheeks and smoothed back her hair. It was the type of gesture that Hannah would have found incredibly embarrassing under other circumstances, but she was so upset about Icky and about her mom leaving that she didn't even protest.

"I'll call you as soon as I can to see how you're doing, I promise," her mom said. "And I'm always just a text, e-mail, or phone call away if you need me."

"I know," Hannah said between sniffles. "I'll miss you, but I'll be okay."

"I know you will," her mom replied firmly. "You're a tough cookie. And Thanksgiving will be here before you know it. When you come visit, we'll eat lots of deep-dish pizza and go to the aquarium, and we'll ride the Ferris wheel at Navy Pier. It will be terrific! And Icky will be home safe and sound well before then, I just know it."

"Bye, Mom," Hannah said after another hug. "Have a good flight."

Hannah watched her mom dash back out in the rain to her car. As soon as she had pulled out of the driveway, Hannah headed back upstairs to her room. Out of the corner of her eye, she caught a flash of Madison in her hot-pink tank top, rounding the corner at the top of the stairs. Hannah's heart sank as she realized that Madison had watched the entire scene between Hannah and her mom, tears and all.

Chapter Five

The next morning, Hannah slept through her alarm and was late getting to the bus stop. She saw the bus pull up when she was still a block away, but she figured Madison would hold it for her. Instead, Hannah made it to the corner just as the driver was closing the door.

"Wait!" Hannah cried, and the door opened again.

"Sorry about that," the driver said kindly. "I didn't see you there."

Thanks a lot, Madison, Hannah thought as she walked toward the middle of the bus. The glare Madison gave her was a pretty good indication that she definitely had *not* tried to hold the bus for her new stepsister.

Hannah slid into the only empty seat she saw, which unfortunately happened to be two seats behind Madison and her best friend, Alexis Schaefer. Hannah heard Alexis's shrill voice waft over the bus seats.

"Ugh," Alexis scoffed. "I can't believe that dork is your stepsister."

"I know," Madison agreed loudly. "You'll never believe what happened yesterday. She spent half the day crying her eyes out over her lost kitty cat, like a six-year-old."

"Seriously?" Alexis asked as she cracked her chewing gum.

Hannah was mortified. She slouched down in her seat and hoped no one around her realized Madison and Alexis were talking about her.

"Can you believe it?" Madison continued. She laughed sharply. "First her mother leaves her, then her cat. What a loser."

Tears sprang to Hannah's eyes. She wasn't usually so emotional, but hearing Madison mention her mom had gotten to her. Hannah knew Madison had a mean streak, but she hadn't expected her to stoop so low. *What have I ever done to her, anyway?* Hannah thought. For once in her life, she couldn't wait to get to school.

Relief flooded through Hannah when she got to homeroom and saw Paisley sitting near the windows.

"I've had the worst morning," Hannah groaned as she slipped into the seat next to her friend. "Come to think of it, yesterday wasn't so hot either."

"What happened?" Paisley asked, concern etched on her face. "Did Icky come home?"

"No, he's still missing." Hannah sighed. "And that's not even the worst of it." She filled Paisley in on Madison's latest mean-girl antics. She almost told Paisley about the scratching sound that had woken her in the middle of the night, too, but for some reason she decided to keep that detail of her miserable weekend to herself. Hannah still wasn't quite sure what had happened, and she didn't want Paisley thinking she was making things up.

Paisley loved talking about local legends, and Hannah knew she even half-believed them, but lying or making things up was another story. The only time Paisley had ever been really angry with Hannah was when they had been five years old. Hannah loved Paisley's favorite stuffed toy, an elephant named

Ellie. Every so often, the girls would swap toys, and Ellie would go to Hannah's house for a sleepover while Hannah's teddy bear, Charlie, stayed at Paisley's.

During one of those stuffed toy sleepovers, Hannah decided she couldn't let Ellie go. His blue elephant fur was the softest she had ever felt, and she loved cuddling up with him. She just had to have him. So she told Paisley that she had lost him. Hannah felt guilty about it the entire time, but she kept that toy for an entire week before her mom found out and returned Ellie to Paisley.

After that, Paisley didn't want to play with Hannah for weeks. Finally, the girls' mothers got them together and convinced them to be friends again. But Hannah still remembered what Paisley had told her after they made up. Paisley had looked Hannah straight in the eye and said, "I don't like friends who tell lies." And Hannah had promised Paisley (and herself) that she would never, ever lie to her friend again.

Hannah knew telling Paisley about the scratching sound wouldn't be lying, but she wasn't sure what Paisley would think. With her mom gone, Hannah couldn't bear the thought of not having Paisley in her life. So she kept the rest of the details of her weekend to herself, just in case.

"I don't understand Madison," Paisley said, shaking her head. "Why is she going out of her way to be so nasty? It's not like you did anything to her. And you're the one who had to move! She could show a little empathy."

"Something tells me Madison got that one wrong on her vocab quiz," Hannah said with a little laugh. "I seriously doubt she even knows what the word means."

"Well, let's focus on the things we can actually do something about," Paisley said reasonably. "Take Icky, for example. We can put up some 'Lost Cat' flyers after school."

"That would be great!" Hannah agreed enthusiastically.

Paisley pulled out her calendar. "Let me just make sure I'm free this afternoon." She flipped through a few pages and frowned.

"I don't get it," she said, finally looking up at Hannah. "I always leave at least one free day per week, but I'm fully booked for the next month! Between soccer, dance, clarinet, student government, and homework, I don't have a single free afternoon."

"Oh," Hannah said softly, trying hard not to show her disappointment. She was used to Paisley's hectic schedule, but her friend always made time to spend with Hannah, too, even if she did have to schedule it in.

Paisley sighed. "I'm sorry, Hannah," she said apologetically. "I guess seventh grade is going to be tougher to manage than I thought."

"That's okay," Hannah said as the bell rang for homeroom to begin. "I'll figure something else out. Maybe my dad will help me hang the flyers."

"Thanks for understanding," Paisley whispered as their homeroom teacher, Mr. Jaffe, began taking attendance. "You're the best!"

Hannah smiled weakly. She didn't feel very understanding. Was seventh grade going to be the year Paisley stopped having time in her schedule for her best friend? That was just one more change Hannah didn't think she could bear.

Hannah slipped into her English class just as the bell rang for first period to begin. It was only after she sat down that she remembered that English was her one class with Madison. Hannah glanced around, breathing a sigh of relief when she didn't spot her evil stepsister. Then something made her turn around.

Madison was sitting right behind Hannah. She scowled darkly.

Great, Hannah thought. *Just when I thought this day couldn't get any worse.*

"Today we're going to talk about legends," their English teacher, Mr. Bonaventure, announced as he paced the front of the classroom. "Can anyone define the term *legend*?"

Everyone was silent. Finally, the class brain, Emilia Lacey, raised her hand.

"It's a story that's passed down from one generation to another, right?"

"Yes, that's part of it," Mr. Bonaventure agreed. "But legends aren't just tales that are passed down within families or among groups of friends — they're stories that become so popular that everyone knows them, even if no one is sure if they're true or not."

"You mean like the legend of King Arthur?" Thomas Lee asked. He was on the fencing team and was really into anything medieval. Hannah's mom had dragged her to the New York Renaissance Faire in August, and Hannah had bumped into Thomas —

literally. He had been wearing a costume with puffy sleeves and he had said something goofy like "Pardon me, m'lady" after almost knocking her over.

"Yes, the legend of King Arthur is a great example," Mr. Bonaventure replied. "Robin Hood is another. Can anyone think of some local legends that originated right here in our area?"

Ryan Walsh raised his hand. "Rip van Winkle?" he asked hesitantly.

"Yes, that's one of them," Mr. Bonaventure said. "Any others?"

Silence again. The answer was so obvious Hannah couldn't believe no one was speaking up.

Without even meaning to, the words popped out of her mouth. "The legend of Sleepy Hollow."

"Yes!" Mr. Bonaventure cried. "That's one of the most famous legends in this town, and we're going to be reading it this week."

The class groaned, and even Hannah rolled her eyes. It wasn't the first time any of them had read "The Legend of Sleepy Hollow" in school. In fact, Hannah's sixth grade English teacher had made the class study the story for an entire month. Every teacher in town obviously thought it was the thing to do during pumpkin season.

"Any other local legends you can think of?" Mr. Bonaventure asked as he passed out copies of the story.

"Well, there are all those ghost legends about the cemetery," Shana Strobert said. "You know, like the story about the ghost cat? People see it around there all the time."

A bunch of the boys laughed. "That's no ghost!" Jordan Saks shouted. "That's just a cat from crazy old Mrs. Wilkinson's house. She's got about a thousand of them in there."

"Yeah, weird people live near the cemetery," Parker Anderson added. "Like that one over there." He gestured at Hannah. "I know cuz I'm on her bus."

Hannah rolled her eyes. Parker had been pestering Hannah regularly since second grade, when he had been known to chase the girls during recess, trying to kiss whichever ones he could outrun. When he'd come after her, Hannah had been so afraid she had panicked and accidentally punched him in the stomach. Even though they'd been seven at the time, Parker had never forgotten. Hannah wasn't sure if it was because Parker had been impressed or annoyed by Hannah, but he always went out of his way to make wisecracks at her expense. By now, she was pretty used to it.

"Thank you for those colorful anecdotes, gentlemen," Mr. Bonaventure said crisply. "And the correct word is *because*, Parker."

Thankfully, the bell rang to end class. As Hannah headed for the door, Parker and his friends jostled past her, knocking one of her books out of her arms.

A second later, Ryan Walsh was standing in front of Hannah, holding out her book.

"Looks like you dropped this," he said, brushing his floppy dark brown hair out of his equally dark brown eyes. "And for the record, I think it's cool that you live near the cemetery. I live pretty close to it, too."

"Um, thanks," Hannah said softly, her cheeks flushed with embarrassment. Or was it something else? She couldn't help but notice how cute Ryan was.

"See ya," Ryan said as he walked out the door.

Hannah practically floated out of the classroom. For some reason, despite everything that had happened that morning, she suddenly felt lighter and happier.

That is, until Madison stepped in front of her. She grabbed Hannah's arm and pulled her into the girls' bathroom.

"Look, let's get a few things straight." Madison crossed her arms angrily and glared at Hannah. "I don't appreciate you drawing attention to the fact that *I* live near the cemetery."

"O-kay," Hannah replied slowly. "But I didn't —"

"Save it." Madison cut her off. "You were the one who mentioned Sleepy Hollow. And then that Parker kid points out that *I* live near the cemetery! That place is super-creepy, and my friends are weirded out enough when they come over. It's not exactly cool to live next to a bunch of dead people."

"Parker wasn't talking about you, he was talking about me," Hannah tried to explain. She couldn't figure out why Madison was getting so upset. Probably no one in class even remembered what Parker had said.

"But you live with me now!" Madison practically shouted. "And I have a reputation to maintain. So keep a low profile. Got it?"

And with that, she whipped around and stormed out, her blond ponytail swinging angrily behind her.

Chapter Six

After the bathroom encounter, Hannah tried to steer clear of Madison as much as possible. It wasn't particularly hard, since Madison didn't seem eager to be in the same room with Hannah either. Madison did conveniently keep forgetting to unlock Hannah's door to the bathroom, which meant Hannah was constantly going downstairs to use the one in the front hallway, rather than risk a confrontation with her stepsister.

On Tuesday, Hannah's dad picked her up after school and drove her around her old neighborhood so she could hang up "Lost Cat" signs on telephone poles. Hannah spent the rest of the night sitting near the phone, hoping it would ring with news about

Icky. By the next afternoon, though, there still hadn't been a single call.

Hannah tried to concentrate on her biology homework. As she began labeling the parts of an animal cell, the chat window popped up on her computer screen.

"Mom!" Hannah cried. It had barely been three days since her mother had left, but Hannah suddenly realized how much she missed her.

Litprof43: Hi, Hannah! Sorry I haven't called.

guitargirl: that's ok. how's chicago?

Litprof43: Not too bad. I start teaching tomorrow. How's school?

guitargirl: fine. icky's still missing, tho. ☹ dad and I put up some flyers yesterday but haven't heard anything.

Litprof43: Good idea! I checked in with the Hendersons and they said they're keeping an eye out for him. I'm sure he'll turn up. You know cats — they've got nine lives!!!

guitargirl: ha ha. they also say that curiosity KILLS them.

Litprof43: Hannah, don't be so morbid. Think positively!

guitargirl: [sigh] u aren't the one living next to a cemetery.

Litprof43: Don't be so dramatic! And give the positive energy a try. It will help — I promise!

guitargirl: yeah yeah, i'll try. miss u. ☹

Litprof43: Miss you too, sweetie. Now go do your homework!

Hannah logged off of the chat window and turned back to her biology assignment. She tapped her pencil against the desk softly as she tried to recall the correct placement of the cell membrane and the cell wall.

Scratch, scratch, scratch.

Hannah leaped out of her chair, her heart pounding. Her pencil flew out of her hand and bounced off the windowpane. The scratching was even louder than it had been the other night, and it had come from right outside the window over her desk.

Hannah glanced out into the yard and saw a flash of black fur streak across the backyard. It looked just like a cat — *her* cat!

"Icky?" she gasped. Could it really be him? What was he doing all the way over on this side of town? Had he followed her to her dad's? Animals always seemed to do that sort of thing in Disney movies.

It seemed so unlikely, though. Hannah's mom's house was at least three miles away. She shook her head in disbelief. It was probably just a stray — maybe even one from the cat lady's house that Jordan Saks had mentioned in English class. Still, Hannah had to be sure. If there was even a chance it was Icky out there, she had to go after him.

Hannah grabbed her jacket off the back of her desk chair and dashed down the stairs and out the kitchen door into the backyard.

"Icky?" she called out tentatively as she ventured toward the back of the yard. She felt foolish as she repeated his name over and over again. There was no sign of a cat anywhere. A soft breeze rustled the leaves of the trees, and Hannah pulled her jacket tighter around her. When she got to the fence at the edge of the yard, she could see the first row of tombstones about fifteen feet away, just inside the cemetery.

Scratch, scratch, scratch.

Hannah whirled around, her heart leaping into her throat. Not the scratching sound again!

"Who's there?" she squeaked, terrified. "Madison? Is that you? This isn't funny!"

The sound had come from behind her, but the whisper of the wind in the trees was the only reply.

Hannah turned to head back to the house. The sun was beginning to slip behind the trees, and she could feel the temperature dropping.

Scratch, scratch, scratch.

"Ack!" Hannah choked, her knees turning to jelly. She was afraid she was about to pass out.

Get ahold of yourself! Hannah thought. This time, the sound had come from beyond the fence, and Hannah was sure she hadn't imagined it. Instinctively, Hannah turned toward the noise and caught a glimpse of a black shadow moving between two of the tombstones. She was sure the shadow had a white-tipped tail, just like Icky.

Hannah took a step closer to the fence that encircled the backyard. She noticed a small latch in the fence. It was a gate! A gate that led into the cemetery.

As scared as she was, Hannah forced herself to take another step forward, closer to the gate. She knew she should have been heading in the opposite direction, back toward the warm and cozy house. After all, didn't something terrible always happen to girls who wandered into cemeteries alone in horror films?

Still, if there was even a chance that Icky was in the cemetery, lost and alone, Hannah had to find him. She tried to convince herself that the cemetery wasn't any different than the backyard — there were just some stone monuments scattered around it.

They're only crumbling old sculptures, Hannah told herself as she pushed the gate open and stepped into the graveyard, trembling with every step. *Just like the ones I saw at the art museum on our class trip last spring.*

She saw a movement out of the corner of her eye and a wave of confidence washed over her. Hannah plunged after the shadow with sudden determination, pushing aside branches and vines as she went.

Hannah gasped.

In front of her was an enormous tree. An undeniably cute stone bench peeked out from underneath the tree, violet and yellow wildflowers growing around its base. A tangle of pretty green vines climbed up the tree and hung across one of the thick, low-hanging branches, creating a picturesque arbor that almost completely concealed the slab of stone.

There was nothing creepy about it. In fact, the bench looked even cozier and more inviting to Hannah than the Van Meters' manicured wooden porch and swing. If the sun hadn't been setting, it would have made the perfect reading nook.

The sun, Hannah thought suddenly. It was getting dark fast. As cute as the stone bench and arbor were, Hannah had no desire to hang out alone in a cemetery after dark.

Hannah glanced around her one last time, looking for any signs of Icky, but she didn't see anything. If he really was out there among the tombstones, she would have to come back to look again during the day. A breeze swept through the cemetery, and a chill washed over Hannah as she hurried to the fence, through the gate, and back to the house.

Hannah woke up suddenly in the middle of the night. Certain that the scratching sound had woken her, she sat up in bed, listening for it for an agonizing ten minutes. Finally, she realized she hadn't heard a thing, though she *did* have to use the bathroom.

Hannah slipped out of bed and crossed the room silently. Then she grabbed the doorknob and twisted it. It was locked.

"Grrr, Madison," Hannah growled under her breath in irritation. She sighed. Now she had to go downstairs in the dark. Hannah stepped into her slippers and headed out of her room and down the stairs. The porch light shone through the front door, illuminating the way with a soft yellow glow. Hannah was careful to move slowly and quietly so as not to wake Allison and her dad, but just as Hannah reached the last step, she heard it.

Scratch, scratch, scratch.

It was coming from the porch.

Hannah froze on the steps, terrified. She couldn't take a step forward, but she didn't want to turn her back to the front door to go back up the stairs either.

And then she saw it — a dark shadow slowly moving across the doorway.

Hannah screamed.

Chapter Seven

In an instant, the lights overhead flicked on, and Allison and Hannah's dad appeared at the bottom of the stairs. Allison was wearing an oversize T-shirt that read I ♥ HULA over a pair of lime-green boxer shorts, and Mr. Malloy was wearing plaid flannel pajamas. If she hadn't been so scared, Hannah might have laughed.

"Hannah!" her dad cried, grabbing her by the shoulders. "What is it?"

"I — I saw a shadow on the porch," Hannah whispered hoarsely, embarrassed that she had woken everyone up, but still shaking from the scare. Madison was lurking at the top of the stairs, her arms crossed, a sleepy scowl on her face.

"And I heard a scratching sound, too," Hannah added, remembering the details. "It sounded like someone was trying to break into the house."

Hannah glanced up at Madison again, fully expecting to see a mean smirk. Instead, Madison's face had suddenly gone white. She looked as though she had seen a ghost.

"What were you doing on the stairs?" Allison asked, perplexed. The scowl returned to Madison's face. Hannah wasn't sure how to explain that Madison had locked her out of the bathroom, so she made up an excuse.

"I, uh, was thirsty and came downstairs to get a drink of water," she said meekly.

Her dad unlocked the front door and stepped out onto the porch.

"Hello?" he called. "Is someone there? I'll call the police!"

His threat hung limply in the air as he stepped back inside a moment later.

"I don't see anyone," he said. "Are you sure it wasn't just a shadow from the trees?"

"Y-yes, I'm sure," Hannah stuttered, her hands still trembling. There weren't even any trees in front of the house — they were all in the backyard. There had definitely been someone — or something — on the porch. Didn't her dad believe her?

Mr. Malloy looked skeptical. "Maybe it was an animal, like a raccoon," he suggested, gently putting his arm around Hannah's shoulder. "They love to get into the trash cans at night. I'll bet that was the noise you heard."

Hannah brushed his arm off her shoulder. Suddenly, she was angry. She could tell from the look on her dad's face that he expected her to just agree with him and admit that it had probably been a raccoon, or a squirrel, or her imagination. Her dad was one of the most reasonable people in the world, and he always assumed there was an explanation for everything. But Hannah knew she hadn't imagined it. There had been something *unnatural* about that shadow.

"Dad, it *wasn't* a raccoon," Hannah insisted stubbornly, her arms crossed defiantly. "There was something else out there — something *weird*. I could tell."

Hannah's dad still looked skeptical, but his face softened a bit. "Well, whatever it was, it's gone now. I say we all head back to bed and try to get some sleep. You girls have school tomorrow."

Too tired to argue, Hannah allowed herself to be escorted back to her bedroom. She climbed into her bed and tried to fall back to sleep, but as soon as she started to doze off, she realized she had never used the bathroom. Even though she figured it was still locked, something made her slip out of bed one more time to try the bathroom door.

For the first time since she had moved in, it was open.

The next morning in homeroom, Hannah was so tired she could barely keep her eyes open. After she had gone back to bed, she had slept fitfully, waking up a few times each hour.

Hannah propped her chin up on her hand and yawned.

"Hannah!" Paisley scolded. "Have you heard a word I just said?"

"Mmmmm," Hannah mumbled. "Something about soccer tryouts . . ." She yawned again.

Paisley shook her head. "You're hopeless, Hannah," she said. "How do you expect to make it through seventh grade if you're not getting enough sleep at night? You'll never be able to keep up with all your activities!"

"I don't have activities," Hannah muttered grumpily through another yawn. "*You're* the one with the fully loaded schedule."

Hannah hadn't meant to sound irritated, but in her sleepy state that's how the words had come out.

"What's that supposed to mean?" Paisley asked, her voice rising the way it did whenever she got upset.

"Oh, nothing," Hannah said offhandedly. "I'm just tired, that's all."

"Well, you don't need to get annoyed with me," Paisley said huffily.

"Seriously, Paisley, I didn't mean anything by it," Hannah said with a sigh. "Don't get so bent out of shape."

"Bent out of shape?" Paisley asked, her voice rising again. "I can't help it if you're jealous of my busy schedule."

Hannah rolled her eyes. "I'm not *jealous*, Paisley," she snapped. "I'm *tired*. I barely slept last night. I —"

Hannah stopped herself. Should she tell Paisley about the shadow on the porch? Or would Paisley think she was just making it up?

Suddenly, the bell rang, piercing Hannah's thoughts before she could say another word.

Paisley picked up her backpack and left the room without saying good-bye.

Hannah shook her head groggily. What had just happened? Had she and Paisley just had an argument? *What had it even been about?* Hannah wondered. She was too tired to fully process any of it. Instead, she dragged herself out of her chair and headed to her English class.

By the end of the day, Hannah was so exhausted she didn't think there was any way she was going to make it through her guitar lesson. She shuffled into the music shop and took a seat in the waiting room, wishing she could curl up on the row of chairs for a quick nap. But just a few minutes later, her teacher, Mr. Gabrielli, who everyone called Mr. G., popped out of his small studio.

"Come on in, Hannah," he said warmly.

She stifled a yawn as she followed him inside.

Hannah took her guitar out of its case and tuned it quickly. Then she began strumming a few of her favorite chords to warm up.

As soon as the lesson began and Hannah started playing, it was as though a weight lifted off her shoulders. She completely forgot about how exhausted she was, and her fingers took over, moving across the strings with confidence and ease.

By the end of the lesson, Hannah was more relaxed and energized than she had felt all day.

"Great job today, Hannah," Mr. G. said. "You played with a lot of feeling, and you're really improving every week. Keep up the good work!"

Hannah blushed at the compliment. "Thanks," she said. "I'm going to practice even more this week if I can."

"Excellent," Mr. G. said. "That's just what you should be doing. You know, every December I organize a recital for all of my students. I know you've been playing for less than a year, but you really should think about performing. You would be fantastic. This year, the recital will be on the tenth."

Hannah's calm and relaxed mood evaporated instantly. Her eyes grew wide with terror.

"No!" she shouted. "I mean, I don't think I can make it that weekend."

Mr. G. looked at Hannah carefully. "Why not?" he asked gently. "Is everything okay?"

"It's just, um, I just, er —" Hannah stuttered, unable to get the words out.

"Yes?" Mr. G. asked expectantly, a kind look on his face.

"I can't play in front of other people," Hannah whispered softly. "I get terrible stage fright. When I was six, I took ballet and I completely froze during the recital. I stood onstage during the entire dance without moving an inch. It was awful!"

Hannah winced just recalling the mortifying scene. It had been the most embarrassing moment of her life.

"After that, I quit dance and promised myself I would never, *ever* perform in front of an audience again."

Mr. G. nodded sympathetically. "That must have been very difficult," he said gently. "But never is a long time to promise not to do something, especially when you're six. You don't have to decide about the recital today, but promise me you'll at least consider it. You still have plenty of time to prepare, so there's no pressure."

"Okay," Hannah agreed reluctantly. She knew she'd never say yes to performing in the recital, but Mr. G. didn't need to know that yet. "I'll think about it."

She stepped back out into the waiting room and noticed a boy in a navy hooded sweatshirt, jeans, and red sneakers waiting for his lesson to begin.

"Oh!" Hannah cried. It was Ryan, from her English class! "I mean, hey." Heat rose to her cheeks, and she knew her face looked like a tomato. A tomato with red hair. Ugh. Why did she have to turn bright red whenever Ryan glanced her way?

"Hey," he said, a warm smile spreading across his face. "I didn't know you took guitar. I haven't seen you here before."

"I just switched my lessons to Thursdays because my dad works late on Tuesdays and can't pick me up," Hannah told him.

"Well, you sounded really good," Ryan said. He seemed impressed. Then he glanced down at his sneakers nervously. "Maybe we can, um, play together sometime."

Hannah tried to open her mouth to say something, but nothing came out, so she just nodded.

"Great!" Ryan said with another smile. "See you in English tomorrow?"

"Um, yeah, see you then," Hannah replied, her vocal cords finally working again.

As she walked outside to wait for her dad, Hannah replayed Ryan's words in her head. Had she really just agreed to hang out and play guitar with him sometime? Her stomach twisted anxiously at the thought, but she decided to put it out of her mind. She had enough to worry about as it was. She had to find Icky, deal with Madison, figure out where the creepy scratching noise was coming from, *and* make up with Paisley after their silly fight. And on top of all that, she had to work on not turning the shade of an overripe tomato the next time she saw Ryan.

Hannah sighed. She wondered if her life would ever be simple and normal again.

Chapter Eight

On Friday, Hannah wanted to talk to Paisley about their argument, but Paisley was called into a special student council meeting. And on Saturday, Hannah and her dad were supposed to go on a bike ride, but Mr. Malloy had to cancel at the last minute because he had to stay home to deal with the contractors while Allison attended a baby shower.

Bored and annoyed, Hannah sat in her room, moping about the canceled bike ride and feeling sorry for herself. She hadn't gotten a single call about Icky yet, which added to her misery. In an attempt to cheer up, she took out her guitar and played a few of her favorite songs. But almost as soon as Hannah began to practice, Madison turned up her stereo and a pounding bass shook the walls of Hannah's room.

Unable to hear her own guitar, Hannah stormed out of her bedroom and knocked loudly on Madison's door. She was so angry that she was determined to finally stand up to Madison, once and for all.

Well, I will if she ever opens the door, Hannah thought dejectedly.

Hannah pounded on the door again, but there was still no answer. Either Madison was ignoring her, or the music was so loud she couldn't hear anything. Hannah even tried the doorknob, but of course it was locked.

She headed back to her room in frustration and put her guitar away. There was no way she could practice over Madison's music. In fact, it was so loud she doubted she would be able to concentrate on anything if she stayed in her bedroom, so she took her English and math books down to the kitchen. With nothing better to do, she figured she might as well get a head start on her homework.

Hannah had just solved her first algebra equation when the sound of an electric drill pierced the relative silence of the kitchen. The drilling was followed by a burst of hammering and another round of drilling. The contractors were obviously hard at work, and they didn't seem concerned about making too much noise.

"I give up!" Hannah yelled to the empty kitchen. It was impossible to concentrate on her homework while she was inside the house, so Hannah thought she'd try working outside. She was about to head for the swing on the front porch when she remembered the stone bench and arbor she had discovered in the cemetery earlier that week.

Hannah weighed her options for a moment — stone bench in creepy but quiet cemetery, or porch swing directly underneath Madison's window (loud, terrible pop music included)?

Hannah headed toward the cemetery gate.

The sun felt warm and pleasant, and in the bright daylight, the cemetery wasn't particularly creepy. Hannah found the tree easily, but the bench was partially obscured by the hanging vines that dangled over the arbor. She pushed aside a few of the vines and settled into her nook. The cemetery was peaceful and quiet, and Hannah finished her algebra homework in record time. Then she pulled out her English assignment, "The Legend of Sleepy Hollow," which they would be discussing in class that week.

Hannah finished the story quickly. She'd read it many times and had never found it particularly scary before. This time was no different, despite the fact that she was sitting in the very cemetery the headless horseman had ridden past. Hannah was proud of herself for overcoming her fear of the cemetery, at least.

She closed her eyes for a minute and was suddenly hit with a wave of sleepiness. The past few nights she hadn't slept well, and her tiredness was catching up to her. She figured it wouldn't hurt to stretch out on the stone bench for a quick catnap.

A second later, she was sitting in her dad's backyard on a lounge chair on a sunny afternoon with Icky in her lap. He was purring loudly as she pet his soft, black head.

Scratch, scratch, scratch.

Icky's ears pricked up as he heard the scratching sound, and he jumped out of Hannah's lap and dashed into the cemetery.

"No, Icky!" Hannah cried. "Wait for me!"

Suddenly, it was nighttime. Hannah ran into the cemetery after Icky, tripping over tombstones and pushing aside dangling vines and cobwebs that kept falling in front of her face or brushing against her bare legs. She stopped running in front of an enormous old mausoleum. It looked like it was made of stone, but when Hannah reached out to touch it, the stone crumbled underneath her fingers as though it was made of sand.

Scratch, scratch, scratch.

The scratching was coming from inside the mausoleum!

Hannah watched in horror as the door began to open slowly. She tried to run, but she looked down to see that vines had wound their way around her ankles and legs, rooting her in place. A spider began climbing up one of the vines and jumped onto her arm.

Hannah screamed.

She gasped as she sat up on the bench, her heart pounding wildly. The nightmare had felt so real Hannah could still feel the spider crawling up her arm. She glanced down and was relieved to see there were no vines or cobwebs wrapped around her legs — it really had been just a dream.

Shaken by the nightmare, Hannah decided it was time to brave a return to the noisy house. But when she entered the kitchen, everything was eerily quiet. Hannah could no longer hear the thumping of

Madison's music through the ceiling, and the hammering and drilling had stopped as well. There were a few brown paper bags full of groceries on the counter and one bag lying on the floor.

"Hello?" Hannah called. "Anyone home?"

She bent down to pick up the paper bag when it suddenly shifted with a soft crinkling sound.

Scratch, scratch, scratch.

The sound had come from behind her, and Hannah whipped around, forgetting about the paper bag. Was someone — or something — at the back door?

She looked out into the backyard but saw nothing. Her pulse was racing as she closed the door and turned back to the paper bag on the floor. It was completely still. Hannah stared at it for a good ten seconds while she gathered up her courage. Finally, she leaned down to try to pick it up again. As soon as she did, the bag skittered across the room.

"Ahhhh!" Hannah yelped, glancing around the kitchen, desperately looking for an open window to explain why the bag had moved. But all of the windows were closed, and Hannah had just closed the back door herself.

Could there be something inside the bag, like a mouse? Allison and her dad *were* doing construction, and Paisley's family had had a mouse in their basement when they re-carpeted, so Hannah knew it was possible. Still, she shuddered at the thought.

At that moment, her dad entered the kitchen.

"Hi, Hannah," he said.

"Shh!" Hannah squeaked, pointing to the paper bag. "I think there's something *in* there! The bag just moved across the floor *by itself*!"

"Okay, relax," Mr. Malloy said calmly. "It's probably just a cricket. I find them around here all the time. That's what happens in an older house." He looked around the kitchen for something to use as a weapon and settled on a large wooden spoon.

Hannah raised her eyebrows skeptically at his choice. "What if it's a mouse, Dad?" she asked, her voice trembling.

He smiled and shrugged. Then he leaned over, reached out slowly, and grabbed the bag at the open end.

Hannah held her breath as she waited to see what was inside.

Her dad held up the bag. It was empty.

Mr. Malloy looked puzzled. "There's nothing in here except the receipt from the store."

Hannah's face went pale. "B-but it moved!" she insisted. "I saw it move!"

Her eyes filled with tears. What was wrong with her? Was she seeing things now, in addition to hearing weird, unexplained noises?

"It's okay, Hannah," her dad said gently. "It was probably just a breeze."

"But, Dad, the windows *aren't even open*," Hannah pointed out, her panicked voice rising.

Mr. Malloy looked as perplexed as Hannah felt.

"Well, maybe it really was a cricket, and it hopped away before I picked up the bag," her dad said. "In any case, I'm going to start dinner. It'll be ready in about an hour."

Hannah headed upstairs to her room, feeling numb. There was one thing she was sure of — there definitely had *not* been a cricket in the paper bag.

Chapter Nine

The next week, Hannah woke up to the scratching noise almost every night. Even when she made it through the night without hearing the awful sound, she slept in a terrified half-sleep. On Tuesday night, Hannah started wearing earplugs in an attempt to block the sound out. She desperately wished Icky were sleeping by her side. At least that would have made her feel safer.

At school, things weren't much better. Hannah could barely stay awake through her classes. The argument Paisley and Hannah had had during homeroom on Thursday had blown over, but things weren't quite the same. Paisley always seemed distracted, and the only time Hannah saw her was in homeroom, since her activities kept her busy after school every day. Hannah suddenly realized how much a part of their friendship their bus rides to and from school had been. But now that Hannah lived on the other side of town, those moments at the beginning and end of each day were a thing of the past.

In addition to the fact that Hannah hadn't had much of an opportunity to talk to Paisley about the mysterious scratching sound even if she had wanted to, she was still reluctant to open up to her friend. Hannah was pretty sure Paisley would believe her, but there was a small sliver of doubt. What if Paisley accused her of making it all up? That would have been too much for Hannah to bear, so she figured it was safer to keep quiet.

The one bright point in Hannah's life was that Madison left her alone for the most part, especially on the bus to and from school. In fact, Madison seemed to have a glazed look in her eyes each morning, as though she wasn't getting much sleep either.

After school on Wednesday, Hannah was in her room, trying to study for a biology test, when she fell asleep at her desk. She woke when a sheet of paper brushed against her face. Hannah shook her head groggily and looked around the room to see sheets of biology notes and her English essay whipping around the room as though a hurricane was passing through. Hannah looked up to find the ceiling fan spinning at top speed. She jumped up and pulled the cord dangling from the fan to turn it off. Then she gathered up her science notes and the pages of her English essay and stacked them neatly on her desk with a sigh. Just when she thought she and Madison had come to some sort of truce, her stepsister had struck again.

That night at dinner, Allison and Mr. Malloy were busy discussing the contractors while Hannah and Madison ate their vegetable stir-fry in silence.

"They're almost done with the walls, so we can pick out paint this weekend, Dan," Allison said eagerly as she passed Hannah the brown rice.

"Mmm-hmmm," Hannah's dad agreed through a mouthful of rice and veggies.

Madison wrinkled her nose. "I hope you're not going to start painting this weekend, Mom," she said. "You know I'm having friends over on Saturday, and Alexis has really bad allergies. She can't be around dust or paint."

Seriously? Hannah thought. *Who's allergic to paint?*

"Don't worry, sweetie," Allison said. "Dan and I have plenty of other things to do on Saturday, so we'll leave the painting for later."

"What about you, Hannah?" Mr. Malloy asked. "Do you have plans this weekend?"

"Um . . ." Hannah hesitated. She didn't have plans yet, but that didn't mean she couldn't have a friend over, too. "Paisley might sleep over on Friday," she said without thinking.

"That sounds nice," Allison said. "Dan, I've heard it's supposed to be warm again on Friday. Remind me to talk to the contractors about fixing the wiring on the ceiling fans. Maybe I can get them to do it tomorrow so the fans are working when Hannah and Madison have their friends over."

"That's a good idea, especially since we just took out all the window air-conditioners last weekend," Mr. Malloy agreed.

Hannah had been only half-listening, but suddenly she was all ears.

"Did you say the fans *haven't* been fixed yet?" Hannah asked.

"Yes, why?" Allison replied.

"Well, my fan's already working," Hannah said, giving Madison a hard look as she did. But Madison didn't flinch. In fact, Hannah was impressed at how clueless she appeared.

Allison set down her fork. "But that's not possible, Hannah," she said, her brow furrowed with concern. "The fans in this house have been broken since I moved in nine years ago. They haven't worked in almost a decade."

Hannah looked at her dad in alarm. He gave her a look that she couldn't quite place. Then Hannah suddenly realized why. She hadn't seen that look in years. It was the one he used whenever he had been certain that Hannah was lying when she was a little girl.

He thinks I'm making it up! Hannah thought. Her heart sank as she realized he probably thought she had made up the stories about the paper bag and the shadow on the front porch, too. Hannah realized she was probably right to not tell Paisley everything that had been going on — if even her dad thought she was lying about it, her best friend would probably think so, too.

"Dad, I promise you, the fan in my room was working before dinner," Hannah said, desperate for him to believe her. "Why would I lie about that?"

"I don't know, Hannah," he said, looking unsure. "I don't think you would, but you've always had a very active imagination. And I know you've been under a lot of stress lately with the move. . . ."

He trailed off.

Ask Madison! Hannah wanted to shout. *She's the one who turned on the fan!* But Hannah took one look at Madison and suddenly knew that the other girl didn't have a clue what was going on. She looked almost as confused as Hannah's dad.

"Just forget it," Hannah said bitterly as she stood up from the table. "I must have imagined it."

Hannah headed up to her room feeling more alone than she ever had in her entire life. She pulled the cord on the ceiling fan, hoping it would work, but it didn't. Then she threw herself facedown on her bed and began to cry into her pillow. She knew if Madison walked in she would never hear the end of it, but at that moment she didn't care.

That night, Hannah fell asleep fully dressed, her face buried in her damp pillow. She was so exhausted from crying that she slept through the night without waking once.

The next morning, Hannah was surprised to find that she actually felt a bit better. The full night of sleep seemed to have done wonders, so she tried hard not to focus on what had helped her sleep so well.

In homeroom, Paisley had to study for a vocabulary quiz because she'd run out of time the night before, thanks to her back-to-back clarinet lesson and soccer practice. Hannah left her alone to study until just before the bell was going to ring.

"Hey, Paisley?" Hannah asked hopefully. "I was wondering if you want to sleep over tomorrow night. We can watch old movies and make caramel popcorn — your favorites."

"Oh, Hannah, I can't," Paisley said distractedly as she closed her vocabulary notebook and slipped it into her backpack. "Indira from soccer is having the entire team over for a spaghetti dinner since we have a big tournament on Saturday. I'm so sorry. Maybe next weekend?"

"Sure," Hannah mumbled, doubtful that Paisley's schedule would be any less busy the following weekend. A second later, the bell rang, and Paisley was gone.

The only thing Hannah was looking forward to for the rest of the day was her guitar lesson. But when she got to the music store after school, she found a hastily written note taped to the door of Mr. G.'s studio. It read:

DEAR STUDENTS:

WAS STRUCK WITH FOOD POISONING AND HAVE TO CANCEL ALL LESSONS THIS AFTERNOON. MY APOLOGIES FOR THE LATE NOTICE. FREE LESSON NEXT WEEK TO MAKE UP FOR IT.

— MR. G.

Hannah felt bad for Mr. G., but she was also annoyed. Why couldn't he have been more careful about what he ate? She had been looking forward to her lesson all week.

Hannah texted her dad and told him the lesson had been canceled and that she would just walk home since she had the extra time. She didn't really want to see her dad, anyway; she was still upset with him for not believing her about the ceiling fan.

Most of Hannah's walk home from the music store was on residential streets and along the occasional commercial strip packed with pizza shops, dry cleaners, and nail salons. But Hannah had forgotten that the last part of the walk was along a long stretch of road that bordered the cemetery. Even though the weather had been super warm lately, it *was* October, and the days were getting noticeably shorter. By the time Hannah got to the cemetery part of the walk, the sun had slipped behind the trees, and the sky had turned a deep, dark blue just barely tinged with pink.

Hannah started up the road quickly, glancing nervously over her shoulder to see if there was anyone else around. The sidewalk and street were both completely empty. There was the occasional *swish* of a car passing by, but other than that, Hannah was completely alone.

The edge of the cemetery was thick with trees, and the leaves cast wild shadows on the sidewalk and on the road in front of Hannah, making her uneasy. It was almost as if the branches were claws that were about to lean over the cemetery fence and pluck her from the sidewalk like a stuffed toy in an arcade game.

It didn't help that some of the leaves had already fallen from the trees, leaving a light coating on the sidewalk. They crackled and crunched under Hannah's boots, piercing the quiet and adding to the creepy scene.

Hannah's heart was beating hard and fast as she walked, and she could hear it pounding in her ears.

The strap on her guitar case dug into her shoulder painfully, but she didn't dare stop to readjust it. She was afraid that pausing even for a second would be an invitation to some ghost or shadow in the cemetery to step out in front of her to say hello.

Hannah could just see the street sign for her block up ahead in the gathering gloom. It was less than thirty feet away. She breathed a sigh of relief and quickened her pace.

Then suddenly, she heard a loud crack behind her, followed by what sounded like footsteps.

Hannah didn't even turn to look — she just broke into a run. When she finally reached the house, she dropped her guitar case with a thud and threw herself into the porch swing with relief, her heart racing and her breathing heavy. Hannah looked down at her hands to see that they were shaking.

Now that she had made it home and was sitting on the peaceful front porch among Allison's pretty flower boxes, Hannah felt silly about her hysterical dash up the street. Still, she *had* heard something behind her. Or had she imagined it? Hannah wasn't even sure she could trust herself anymore.

Chapter Ten

On Saturday morning, Hannah woke to bright sunshine streaming through her window. The scratching sound hadn't woken her for two nights in a row, and the good weather and the fact that it was Saturday filled Hannah with a burst of unexpected optimism. *Maybe the strange noises are gone for good*, she thought hopefully.

Hannah headed downstairs for breakfast. Her dad was sitting at the kitchen table, eating a bowl of cereal and reading the newspaper. Hannah helped herself to a bowl and a spoon and joined him at the table. She poured herself some Cheerios and looked at her dad.

"So, what are you up to today?" Hannah ventured. Her good mood made her eager to forgive him for not believing her the other night. At this point, she wasn't even sure herself whether she had imagined the working ceiling fan or not. "Want to go for a hike?"

Her dad put down his paper. "Oh, Hannah, I wish I could, but I promised Allison we'd go to Home Depot to pick out paint colors for the bedroom and the office today."

"Oh," Hannah said softly. She was disappointed, and her first instinct was to mope about it like she had been doing for the past two weeks. But then something inside Hannah shifted. Suddenly, she didn't want to feel sorry for herself anymore.

I will not *mope around on a beautiful, sunny Saturday*, she thought. She was tired of waiting around for Paisley and her dad to make room in their schedules for her. Today, she was going to do whatever she wanted to do, even if she had to do it alone.

"You don't want to hang out with your boring old dad, anyway, do you?" Hannah's dad asked with a goofy wink. "Didn't Madison say something about having some girlfriends over today? I'm sure you'd much rather do manis and pennies with the girls than go for a hike with your dear old dad."

Hannah rolled her eyes. "It's manis and *pedis*, Dad," she corrected him. Suddenly feeling bold, she continued, "And I don't think Madison would really want me hanging out with her and her friends. In case you haven't noticed, we don't exactly get along."

Hannah's dad looked up at her, a startled expression on his face.

"Er, no, I didn't realize that," he said. Hannah thought he looked extremely uncomfortable. "But I'm sure it's just an adjustment period you girls are going through. I'll bet by Thanksgiving, you'll be great friends!"

He patted her on the hand awkwardly.

"Sure, Dad," Hannah replied, her urge to express her true feelings evaporating as quickly as it had come on. What was the point if her dad wasn't even going to try to understand? "Whatever you say."

Hannah stood up from the table, put her empty cereal bowl in the sink, and headed back upstairs to her room.

Half an hour later, Hannah had a plan. She definitely didn't want to hang out around the house all day, where she would be likely to run into Madison and her friends. So she packed a lunch, her guitar, a fleece blanket, and a book, and she headed out to the backyard. Her cozy little arbor in the cemetery would be the perfect spot to read, play a few songs, and relax.

Hannah was halfway across the yard, heading toward the gate to the cemetery, when, out of the blue, Madison appeared in front of her, blocking her path.

"What the —" Hannah gasped as she stumbled backward, almost dropping her guitar. "Where did you come from?"

"Right over there. I was watching." Madison gestured to the lawn behind her, where three lounge chairs were set up in a circle in the sun, a pile of magazines and a jumble of nail polish bottles lying in the grass between the chairs. Madison crossed her arms across her chest and glared at Hannah menacingly.

"And just where do you think you're going?" Madison demanded.

Hannah took a step back instinctively. But then another wave of self-confidence washed over her.

"That's none of your business," Hannah snapped back. "Now if you don't mind —" She gestured for

Madison to move out of the way so she could pass. Madison looked taken aback that Hannah had actually stood up to her, but it didn't take her long to recover.

"Actually, I *do* mind." Madison narrowed her eyes at Hannah. "Because it looks to me like you're headed for the cemetery, and that is *not* okay with me."

Madison stabbed Hannah in the chest with her index finger. "I *told* you to keep a low profile about that," Madison hissed. "I have friends coming over, and if they see my freaky stepsister running around between the tombstones, it's not going to look good for me."

Madison flipped her blond hair over her shoulder. "Do you have any idea how hard it was to even get my friends to agree to come over here today? They hate the idea of hanging out at my house, but I finally convinced them the cemetery is no big deal. And I'm not going to let *you* ruin everything!"

Now it was Hannah's turn to glare at Madison. She couldn't believe that she had been scared of her before — Madison was just an insecure bully!

"Well, what better way to prove to your friends that the cemetery is harmless than for them to see me hanging out around it?" Hannah asked innocently.

"Harmless?" Madison was aghast. "It's a cemetery! There are bats that fly around at night, and crumbling old tombstones, and mangy stray dogs and cats that live there." She lowered her voice and paused dramatically. "And there are *ghosts*. Bad ones."

Even though it was warm in the sun, Hannah shivered.

"You do know about the ghost cat, right?" Madison asked.

Hannah nodded mutely. Just when she had convinced herself the scratching sounds and the weird things that had been happening had been in her imagination, she had to listen to yet another cemetery ghost story.

"Well, they say that little girl died because her cat lured her to her death," Madison said, her voice barely a whisper. "And people around here have seen the shadow of a black cat in the cemetery. Anyone who follows the shadow is led to their death. When I was eight, there was this little boy, Jeffrey, who lived down the block. One day he wandered into the cemetery alone and got lost in the woods for three days. When they finally found him, he was so dehydrated he almost died. After a few weeks in the hospital, he pulled through, but his family left Sleepy Hollow and never came back. Jeffrey had told his parents that he was following a black cat when he got lost."

Hannah gasped in spite of herself. Could it be true? This version of the story was a lot creepier than the one Paisley had told her.

Madison had a smug, satisfied look on her face.

Hannah was just about to reconsider her plan for the day when she suddenly realized what was going on: Madison was just trying to scare her away from the cemetery for her own purposes. She was probably making up the whole thing about Jeffrey.

Just like earlier, something inside Hannah shifted. She was suddenly angry. Madison had done nothing but make Hannah's life miserable since she'd moved in, and now that Hannah was trying to escape — to a cemetery, of all places! — Madison was trying to stop her from doing that, too.

"Well, you can believe whatever you want, but I *like* the cemetery," Hannah challenged. Her words were punctuated by a burst of drilling noises from the house, indicating that the contractors had started their work for the day. "It's peaceful, quiet, and *relaxing* there. Now, if you'll excuse me, I have a date with a ghost."

Madison's mouth dropped open in shock, and the look on her face was one Hannah would remember for a long time. Hannah felt another surge of confidence rush through her as she strode past Madison, her head high, and headed for the cemetery gate.

"Suit yourself," Madison shouted after her. "But don't say I didn't warn you!"

With Madison and the noisy house finally behind her, Hannah smiled. She headed straight for the cozy little arbor and found it had been undisturbed since her last visit.

Hannah used the blanket to make a cushion on the stone bench, and then settled in to read her book. After just a few chapters, the warm sun caused her to drift off to sleep. In her dream, Hannah stumbled through her mom's house, searching desperately for Icky. She felt a rising panic in her chest as she followed the crying sound from room to room. But every time Hannah got close to Icky, the crying stopped and began again a few seconds later, but from somewhere else.

Just as she was looking for her cat in another room, Hannah woke with a start. Her book slipped off her lap and crashed to the ground. As she leaned down to pick it up, she heard a soft meow behind her. Hannah jumped up and whirled around. Had she really just heard a meow, or had it been part of her dream?

Sure enough, there was another soft meow, and it definitely sounded like it was coming from the other side of the bench. Hannah pinched her arm hard to make sure she was awake. It sounded just like Icky had in her dream! Could he have made it all the way across town to the cemetery?

Hannah leaped up and moved instinctively toward the sound. She took a few steps forward and then stopped to listen. The meow came again, but it sounded even farther away and in the opposite direction. She took off after it.

Hannah continued to follow the sound to the edge of the cemetery and into the surrounding trees. Every time she thought she was getting closer to the cat, though, the meowing shifted and moved farther away.

And then she saw it — a shadowy black tail with what looked like a white patch on the tip.

"Icky!" Hannah cried. She dashed after the shadow, but her toe caught on the gnarled root of a nearby tree. Hannah tumbled forward and landed hard, scraping her palms and skinning her knee against the rough tree root.

Hannah winced in pain as she stood up and brushed off her clothes. She wasn't badly hurt, but she felt silly for chasing after a cat that had probably been just one of the cemetery strays. She turned to head back to her little arbor, but she didn't see tombstones anywhere. All she saw around her were trees.

That's when it hit her.

She was alone in the woods. Alone and completely lost.

Chapter Eleven

Hannah felt her chest tighten with fear. She recalled Madison's story about the little boy who had wandered the woods for three days. Hannah's head began to spin, and she thought she might pass out. She took a deep breath.

"Calm down, Hannah," she told herself aloud. "This is no big deal."

She was a pretty experienced hiker, and she hadn't gone *that* far into the woods. It couldn't be that difficult to find her way back to the cemetery.

Hannah sat down on a nearby tree stump for a moment to collect her thoughts. She closed her eyes and breathed deeply, getting her nerves under control. The woods were quiet except for the breeze rustling the trees and the chirping of a few birds. But then Hannah heard something else. It was a soft swishing sound.

A car! Hannah realized. She jumped up and her eyes flew open. It was the rushing sound of a car on asphalt. A second later, Hannah heard the strains of a faraway police siren. Both sounds were coming from just up ahead. It had to be a road.

Hannah began to move slowly through the woods. Every few steps, the road sounds grew louder and louder. After just a few minutes, she could see the cars through the trees.

"Yes!" Hannah yelled out loud. She pushed aside some vines and squeezed between two small bushes until she was standing on the side of an unfamiliar-looking stretch of road. She didn't see the cemetery anywhere, and there was only one house within view. Hannah headed toward it. She hoped someone could tell her what street she was on so she could find her way home.

As Hannah walked toward the house, she saw a boy and a girl playing basketball in the driveway.

"No way!" the boy yelled. "You were over the line, Taylor."

Hannah stopped short. The boy's voice sounded

familiar. He dribbled the basketball twice and then lobbed it toward the basket. It sliced through the net silently, a perfect shot.

"Yeah!" he yelled as he did a funny jig. "Nothing but net, baby!"

Then he turned and noticed Hannah standing at the end of the driveway. Hannah recognized him immediately. This time, he was the one whose cheeks turned tomato red.

"Oh, hey," Ryan mumbled. "Did you see that?"

Hannah couldn't help but smile. "Yeah," she said. "Nice shot."

"Er, I meant my victory dance," he said. Even the tips of his ears were pink.

Hannah laughed. "Yup, saw that, too. It was very, uh, original."

Ryan laughed. "Have you met my sister, Taylor?" He pointed to the girl who was now holding the basketball. She had short blond hair, a big smile, and she looked a lot like a female version of Ryan.

"Hi," Hannah said, looking from one to the other. "Are you —"

"Twins?" Taylor finished. "How could you tell?"

Suddenly, Ryan took in Hannah's scraped palms, skinned knee, and dirty T-shirt.

"Whoa, Hannah, what happened?" he asked, a concerned look on his face. "Are you okay?"

Hannah glanced down at her clothes. Her shirt was torn and muddy, and her palms were speckled with bloody scratches. She suddenly remembered how she had ended up at Ryan and Taylor's house.

"Oh, yeah," she replied. "I was just going for a hike behind my house, and I tripped and fell. And I, uh, also got a little turned around. That's how I ended up here."

"Do you want to clean your hands and put on some bandages?" Taylor asked. "Our mom's a nurse, so she's good at this kind of stuff. Come on."

Hannah followed Taylor into the house, where Taylor and Ryan's mom kindly cleaned her palms and knee and put gauze and medical tape over the cuts and scrapes.

"There you go," Mrs. Walsh said sweetly as she secured the last piece of tape. "Good as new."

"Thanks so much," Hannah said. "Do you mind if I use your phone and call my dad? He's probably wondering where I am."

"Of course not," Mrs. Walsh said. "There's a phone in the kitchen. And when you're done, you're welcome to stay for lunch."

Hannah's stomach rumbled loudly at the word "lunch." It seemed like it had been ages since she had packed a sandwich and apple and taken them out into the cemetery that morning. She realized she was ravenous.

"That sounds great," Hannah agreed.

After a lot of explaining, Hannah hung up with her dad. At first, he had been angry that she had gone for a hike on her own, but she explained that she hadn't meant to go so far, and she hadn't meant to get so turned around either. She hadn't mentioned the cat at all — she knew her dad wouldn't believe her even if she had. Finally, he had let her go when she promised Taylor or Ryan would walk her home after lunch.

Ryan came into the kitchen just as Hannah was hanging up the phone.

"There's a peanut butter, banana, and jelly sandwich out on the porch with your name on it," he told her.

"Mmmm, that sounds so good!" Hannah said as she followed him outside.

Ryan poured her a glass of lemonade and handed her a plate with a sandwich and a pile of potato chips on it.

"This sandwich is my specialty," he said proudly. "Usually I put the potato chips in there, too, for some extra crunch, but Taylor made me leave them out of yours in case you thought that was too weird." He shot his sister a look.

"What?" Taylor asked. "It's gross, Ryan. I like to eat my potato chips on the side, like most people. I thought Hannah might feel the same way."

Hannah laughed. "Well, I usually *do* eat my potato chips on their own, but I've also never put banana in my PB&J, so I'm willing to give it a try."

She pulled off the top piece of bread and added a layer of chips before replacing the bread. Hannah picked the sandwich up and took a big bite. She chewed and crunched thoughtfully before making up her mind.

"Taylor, I respect your position on keeping the chips out of the sandwich, and thank you for leaving the decision up to me," Hannah said. "But, Ryan, I'm with you. It's super good!"

"Yes!" Ryan yelled. He jumped up and did his goofy victory dance again.

Taylor rolled her eyes at her brother, but smiled at the same time.

"I call it the PBBPC&J," Ryan said.

Hannah laughed. "That's a mouthful. Maybe you should try something simpler, like the Walsh Special."

Ryan stroked his chin thoughtfully. "Hmmm," he mused. "An interesting suggestion. I'll definitely consider it."

After lunch, Taylor had a piano lesson, so Ryan offered to walk Hannah home.

"Thanks for coming with me," she said. "I feel silly for not knowing the way, but I got so turned around in the woods, and I haven't lived around here long."

"No problem," Ryan said. "I don't mind. Anyway, it's fun hanging out with you."

Hannah felt a little flutter in her stomach. Maybe adding the chips to her sandwich hadn't been such a good idea.

"You know," Ryan continued, "we could hang out even more if you joined my band. I really like to play bass, but I can't unless there's someone else to play lead guitar. And you're really good."

Now Hannah felt something else in her stomach — a knot of nerves.

"I'm not really good at performing in front of people," she admitted.

"Yeah, it can be a little scary, but it gets easier," Ryan said with a shrug. "Plus, Taylor's in the band —

she plays the keyboard and sings. She would really love to have another girl to hang out with during rehearsals. Our cousin Jake is the drummer, and sometimes the two of us kinda take over with our jokes and boy stuff."

Hannah didn't know what to say. She was flattered that Ryan had invited her to join the band, but she was still paralyzed by stage fright. She had never really cared much one way or the other whether she ever performed in front of people again, but suddenly she wished she could.

"Just think about it," Ryan said, sounding just like Mr. G. "You don't have to decide right now."

"Okay, thanks," Hannah said with a tiny sigh of relief. "I'll let you know."

They rounded the corner and Hannah saw her dad's house up ahead.

"Well, that's it." Hannah pointed to the house. "So I guess I can make it the rest of the way from here."

She shifted nervously from her left foot to her right. Now that they had stopped walking, Hannah felt incredibly awkward.

"Right," Ryan said. Hannah thought he looked nervous, too, but maybe it was just her imagination.

Finally, he raised his hand and gave Hannah a small wave. "See you on Monday?"

Hannah nodded. Then she headed toward the house. For some reason, she couldn't seem to stop smiling.

Chapter Twelve

As soon as Hannah had checked in with her dad and reassured him the scrapes and cuts on her hands and knee were no big deal, she went out to the cemetery to retrieve her guitar and the rest of the things she had left there. Luckily Madison and her friends weren't in the yard — their lounge chairs had been abandoned, though there were still nail polish bottles and cotton balls littered all around.

When Hannah got to the arbor, she found everything exactly where she had left it. Well, everything except the fleece blanket. Thinking the wind had lifted the blanket and tossed it somewhere nearby, Hannah circled the tree twice trying to find it, but it was gone.

She considered staying out in the cemetery a bit

longer, but the sky had clouded over and it looked like it was about to rain. So Hannah headed back inside and up to her room. She sat down at her desk and opened her video chat and e-mail. The first message in her in-box was from her mom.

To: guitargirl@cranehost.net
From: Litprof43@cranehost.net
Saturday 11:23 A.M.

Hi, Hannah!
How's everything? My classes are going really well. How about yours? I spoke to your dad yesterday and he said Icky is still on the lam . . . I don't know what's gotten into that cat! I really hope he reappears soon.

What are you doing this weekend? Are you and your dad going on a big hike or bike ride? The leaves are starting to turn here, so I'll bet it's really pretty there right now, too. I always love this time of year! Miss you bunches!

Hugs and kisses,
Mom

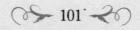

Reading her mom's e-mail made Hannah feel both better and worse at the same time. It was nice to hear from her mom, but it had also reminded Hannah of Icky. The more time that passed, the more Hannah was losing hope that Icky was ever going to find his way home. She still hadn't even gotten a single call from any of the lost cat flyers she and her dad had hung around town.

A soft *ping* interrupted Hannah's thoughts. It was an incoming Skype call from Paisley. Hannah clicked to accept, and Paisley's face filled the screen. She looked exhausted.

"Hi!" Hannah said. "How was your soccer tournament?"

"Terrible," Paisley groaned. "We played four games and lost three. I'm so sore I can barely move."

"Oh no!" Hannah said sympathetically. "That stinks, Pais."

Paisley sighed. "It's okay — I'll live. I'm really sorry I couldn't sleep over last night. That would have been nice. I miss hanging out with you."

"I miss hanging out with you, too," Hannah replied. She wondered if maybe this would be a good time to tell Paisley about the creepy stuff that had been happening to her lately, and maybe even about

Ryan. Just as she was about to open her mouth, Paisley let out a huge yawn.

"Oh, sorry, Hannah," Paisley apologized. "I am so exhausted. I didn't get home from the spaghetti dinner until pretty late last night, and our first game was at eight this morning. I think I need to go take a nap." Paisley yawned again.

"Okay," Hannah said with a soft sigh. Suddenly, it didn't seem like the best time to confide in her friend. She would have to wait until Paisley wasn't so exhausted. "Give me a call tomorrow if you have a chance. If not, I'll see you in homeroom Monday."

That night, a huge thunderstorm rolled in. Lightning lit up Hannah's room, and she tried not to think about Icky huddled under a stranger's porch somewhere in the rain. The earth-shaking cracks of thunder were the kind that typically sent him into hiding under Hannah's down comforter. Icky hated thunderstorms, and Hannah couldn't imagine how he might be coping if he was stuck outside in a storm like this.

After lying awake in bed for more than an hour, Hannah finally drifted off to sleep.

She was alone on a tiny wooden rowboat in the middle of an enormous body of water. Hannah scanned the horizon but couldn't see land anywhere. It was pitch-black outside, and the water was eerily calm and quiet — too quiet. Suddenly, a bolt of lightning lit up the sky, followed by an enormous crash of thunder a few seconds later.

The boat began to pitch wildly back and forth in the waves as the sky opened up and big, fat warm raindrops pelted Hannah and the boat. She grabbed the oar and tried to row somewhere — anywhere — but there was still no land in sight.

"Help!" Hannah cried desperately. But the wind caught the word and it seemed to drift upward and away to a place where no one would ever hear it. The louder she tried to scream, the softer her voice sounded.

Suddenly, Madison was sitting next to her. Hannah gasped and moved backward until she was pressed up against the edge of the boat. Madison threw back her head and laughed. Then she stood up and started to rock the boat harder.

"Stop!" Hannah shouted, but nothing came out of her mouth. She squeezed her eyes shut and willed Madison to sit down. Suddenly, the rain stopped and the rocking slowed until everything was still and quiet. When Hannah opened her eyes again, Madison was gone. In her place, there sat a black cat with bright green eyes. The cat narrowed its eyes at Hannah and began to purr loudly.

Hannah gasped and sat straight up in bed, her heart pounding. It was after midnight. The rain outside had slowed, but she could still hear the *tap-tap-tap* of raindrops dancing on the roof. Then Hannah heard something else. It was the sound of running water.

Madison must be in the bathroom washing her hands, she thought. But after a few minutes, the running water hadn't stopped. *No one washes their hands for that long*, Hannah thought. Curious, she got out of bed and walked toward the bathroom. She pressed her ear up against the door and listened carefully.

The running water was much louder and sounded heavier than the sink. In fact, it sounded as though someone was filling the bathtub.

"Leave it to Madison to decide to take a bubble bath at midnight," Hannah muttered to herself as she shook her head and climbed back into bed. Within a few minutes, she drifted back into a dreamless sleep.

Scratch, scratch, scratch.

Hannah woke a second time. The scratching sound was back! She looked at the illuminated clock on her bedside table. More than ten minutes had passed and the water in the bathroom was still running. Fear washed over her. Something wasn't right.

Hannah got out of bed again and knocked loudly on the bathroom door. No answer. She jiggled the doorknob with trembling fingers, but it was locked.

"Madison?" Hannah called. "Are you in there?"

There was still no answer.

Hannah went out into the hallway and pounded on Madison's door.

"Madison!" she called. "Open up!"

Hannah heard footsteps, and the door flew open to reveal a very groggy — and dry — Madison.

"What do you want?" she snapped angrily. "This better be good. You woke me up!"

Hannah cocked her head toward the bathroom door. She could still hear the water running.

"Do you hear that?" Hannah asked, panic rising in her chest. "The water's been running for, like, ten minutes. I thought you were in there taking a bath, but . . ."

She trailed off.

Madison's eyes widened in terror as she ran over to the bathroom door and turned the doorknob. It didn't open.

Madison looked at Hannah. "It's locked," she said.

Hannah grabbed the doorknob and tried it herself, but Madison was right — the doorknob didn't budge.

"Mine's locked, too," Hannah whispered.

"What do you mean?" Madison asked, anger flashing in her eyes. "Is this some kind of sick joke?"

Hannah shook her head mutely, unable to speak. Just like with the ceiling fan, it was clear that Madison didn't have a clue what was going on. Plus, there was no way she could have locked the bathroom door from the outside.

Madison stormed out of her bedroom and crossed the hallway to Hannah's room.

"What are you doing?" Hannah whispered as she followed Madison.

"Proving that you're a liar who's trying to play a trick on me," Madison said over her shoulder.

"But I swear I didn't —"

Madison whirled around. Hannah had never seen her look so ferocious. "Save it," she snapped. "I know

you're just trying to get back at me because I forgot to unlock your bathroom door a few times *by
accident.*"

Madison stomped through Hannah's bedroom
and stopped in front of the bathroom door.

Hannah couldn't believe what she was hearing.
"Come on, Madison," she implored. "I know those
weren't acci —"

Hannah went mute as she watched Madison
reach out and turn the bathroom doorknob.

It clicked open and gave way easily.

Chapter Thirteen

Hannah gasped. "It was locked, Madison!" she insisted. "I swear!"

Madison rolled her eyes. She crossed her arms across her chest and glared at Hannah. "Nice try," she said. "I knew you were a liar. Now if you don't mind, I'm going back to bed. I know *you* might not care about your looks, but *I* need my beauty rest."

And with that, Madison turned on her heel and stomped back to her room, slamming the door behind her.

Hannah held her breath as she stepped into the bathroom, her heart pounding. She was sure she was going to find a dead cat — or worse — in the tub.

But the only thing in the bathtub was water. It had just reached the top and was starting to spill over onto the floor.

Hannah snatched a towel off the rack and threw it down to soak up the puddle. Then she leaned over and turned off the water with trembling hands.

"Hannah?" a voice behind her asked.

"AHHHHH!" Hannah jerked backward and her foot slid on the wet towel, sending her crashing to the floor.

Her dad, who had called her name from the doorway, rushed into the bathroom.

"Are you okay?" he asked as he helped her up.

Hannah was trembling from the scare, and her teeth were chattering.

"I'm f-f-fine," she managed to choke out as she rubbed her hip, which would undoubtedly be bruised the next day.

Her dad looked baffled. "What's going on up here?" he asked. "Allison and I heard you and Madison yelling, then there were lots of loud footsteps and a door slammed." He paused and glanced at the full-to-the-brim bathtub. His face wrinkled in further confusion. "Isn't it a bit late for a bath?"

Hannah didn't know what to say. All she wanted

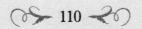

to do was confess everything to her dad and have him tell her it was all going to be all right, but for the first time in her life, she realized her dad couldn't make things better. It wasn't just that she knew her dad wouldn't understand what a mean girl Madison was — it was all the other crazy stuff that had been happening, too. Hannah was sure she was being haunted by something in — or near — the house, and she just knew her dad would think her theory was outrageous.

"Um, Madison and I had a fight," Hannah lied. She was surprised at how easily the story came to her. Maybe she really *was* a natural liar. "I woke her up by mistake, and she got really angry, which made me upset, too. I couldn't fall asleep again, so I thought a bath might help me relax."

Hannah's dad looked at her skeptically, but he just shrugged.

"Well, I'm sorry I startled you," he said sheepishly. "Try to make the bath quick so you can get to sleep."

"Okay, Dad," Hannah replied softly. "Good night."

"You too, Hannah," he replied.

As soon as her dad had gone, Hannah drained the tub and headed back to her bed. She was so exhausted that the second she pulled the covers up, she fell into a deep, dreamless sleep.

When Hannah finally woke up the next morning, the sun was shining brightly outside her window. She rolled over to look at her clock and was shocked to see that it was almost noon.

Hannah got out of bed and headed straight for the bathroom, where she splashed some cold water on her face. Even though she had gotten plenty of sleep, she felt groggier than usual. She was also sore all over from her two falls the previous day — first in the woods and then in the bathroom.

After she pulled on a long-sleeved T-shirt and a pair of jeans, Hannah realized she was ravenous, so she headed down to the kitchen. Unfortunately, Madison was already perched at the table, reading a magazine and drinking a smoothie.

Hannah ignored her as she popped a bagel in the toaster and sat down. The silence in the room was so thick Hannah could have cut it with her butter knife. When her bagel finally popped out of the toaster, she was relieved to have something to do. She quickly spread some cream cheese on the bagel and carried it out to the front porch. It was chilly outside, but even if she caught a cold, Hannah thought it would be a small price to pay for a Madison-free breakfast.

Hannah had just taken her first bite of bagel when there was a large crash inside the house, followed by a shout that sounded like her dad. Hannah jumped up and raced into the house. It sounded as though the noise had come from the garage that Allison and her dad had been remodeling into a home office.

Hannah burst into the garage to find Madison already there, kneeling next to her dad, who was lying in a pool of blood next to a ladder.

"Dad!" Hannah shrieked as she dashed to his side, her face pale and taut with worry. "What happened? Where are you hurt? What's bleeding?" She had never seen so much blood before in her life.

Her dad sat up quickly and held out his red hand. "Relax, Hannah!" he said reassuringly. "It's just paint. See?"

He pointed to a tray of red paint and a red-stained roller brush.

Hannah heaved a sigh of relief. She looked around the room more carefully and noticed the wall to her left was half-covered in the same burgundy color as the floor.

Hannah glanced over at Madison. From the look on her face, it was clear she'd also thought the paint had been blood.

"I'm sorry, girls," Mr. Malloy said sheepishly. "I didn't mean to scare you. I was on the ladder painting when I thought I felt something brush against my legs." He shook his head. "I don't know what came over me. It was almost as though — oh, you girls are going to think I'm a crazy old man!"

"Why, Dad?" Hannah asked urgently, suddenly alert. "What happened?"

Mr. Malloy looked embarrassed as he continued his story. "Well, it was almost as if a cat had brushed against my ankles. It felt just like Icky used to when he was trying to get my attention. There was something soft and furry and — I don't know. But there was nothing there — it must have been my imagination." He chuckled nervously. "I guess I panicked. I just slipped and fell off the ladder."

Hannah and Madison exchanged glances and a moment of understanding passed between them before Madison quickly looked away. Hannah couldn't quite figure out what it had been about Madison's expression that had tipped her off, but something suddenly clicked.

She knows! Hannah realized with a start. *Madison knows that weird things have been happening around here lately!* All of the pieces fell into place: the exhausted look on Madison's face each morning, her warnings about the cemetery, even the locked bathroom door. Hannah realized that Madison must have heard the scratching sound at night, too. And maybe her warnings about the ghost cat and about keeping a low profile around the cemetery had been just that — warnings. Hannah wasn't even sure it had always been Madison locking her bathroom door — it could have been a ghost!

Hannah shuddered at the thought.

She glanced around the room looking for signs of a ghost, and she saw something that made her blood run cold.

Suddenly, she was certain beyond a doubt that there was something — or someone — much scarier than Madison in her dad's house.

Hannah helped her dad stand up. As she did, she moved so that she blocked his view of the evidence she had just spotted.

"That's okay, Dad," she said, a false note of cheer in her voice. "You didn't scare us too badly, and I'm glad you're not hurt."

For some reason, Hannah didn't want her dad to know about the ghost. She didn't think there was any way he'd ever believe it. And now that she was sure something strange was happening, she didn't think she could take all of his "it's just your imagination" theories.

"It's a good thing Allison convinced me to leave the floor installation for last," Mr. Malloy said as he glanced at the paint-splattered garage floor. It looked about as bad as his T-shirt and jeans, which were covered in enormous globs of red paint. "I'm just going to go change out of these clothes."

"Great idea!" Hannah said, a little too eagerly. She practically pushed him back into the house. "Madison and I can start cleaning up some of this paint for you."

Madison shot Hannah one of her poison-dart glares as Mr. Malloy disappeared through the garage door.

"And *why* would we do that?" she asked snippily.

"Because of that," Hannah said, pointing to the floor behind her.

Madison gasped.

There was a trail of tiny paw prints — *cat* paw prints — leading away from the puddle of paint. The prints didn't seem to go anywhere — they just got

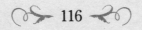

fainter and fainter as they neared the exterior wall of the garage, until they finally faded away.

Hannah grabbed a rag and splashed some paint thinner on it. Then she knelt down and began scrubbing at the prints. Madison took a rag from the pile and did the same thing.

"Have you heard it?" Hannah asked Madison softly as they scrubbed. "The scratching at night?"

Madison looked up, alarmed. Her face had gone pale. But she just put her head down and scrubbed harder.

"Come on, Madison," Hannah pleaded. "You know what I'm talking about — I can tell! I know you've heard it, too."

"I don't know what you're talking about," Madison replied, but Hannah had seen Madison stiffen when she mentioned the scratching.

"It's the ghost cat," Hannah insisted. As soon as she said it aloud, she knew it was true. She turned to Madison. "You didn't turn on the fan in my room or run the water in the bathtub, did you?"

Madison shook her head, her eyes wide with fear. "No, I told you I didn't," she replied carefully.

"Well, I didn't do it either, but someone — or some*thing* — did," Hannah said firmly. "The ghost cat is haunting me. It's haunting *us*. Admit it, Madison. You know it's true!"

"I don't want to talk about it," Madison snapped. "If it gets around at school that I'm being haunted, no one will want to hang out with me! No one will ever want to sit with me at lunch again. So we're not talking about it — and you're not telling anyone about it either — *ever*."

But Hannah desperately wanted to talk to Madison about the ghost cat. Finally, here was someone who believed her! It didn't matter how mean Madison had been to Hannah when she had first moved in — now they had something in common, and Hannah needed her help. She was certain that if she and Madison worked together, they could figure out a way to get the haunting to stop. And Hannah *had* to figure out a way to make it stop — she didn't think she could live in a constant state of fear much longer.

"But if we just talk about it, maybe we can figure out what to do," Hannah said desperately. "We have to do *something*."

Madison gave Hannah one of her famous icy stares. The only difference was that this time, Madison looked scared to death.

"I told you — I don't want to talk about it!" she shouted. Then she jumped up and dashed out of the room, almost knocking Hannah down in the process.

Hannah threw down her rag in frustration. She felt more alone than ever.

A moment later, her dad reappeared.

"Much better!" he said happily as he stepped into the room wearing a hideous pair of paint-splattered denim overalls over a stained plaid shirt. "Forgot I had these old work overalls in the back of my closet."

Hannah gave him a weak smile. "Very stylish, Dad," she said. "I'm going to bike to the library to do some research. I, uh, have a big history report to work on."

"Sure, no problem," her dad replied distractedly. He had already started painting again. "But wear a jacket — it's getting chilly out there!"

The part about the history report had been a little white lie, but Hannah figured she had already been accused of being a liar, and it wasn't the first one she had told either. It was clearly time to take matters into her own hands. She was going to get to the bottom of the ghost cat haunting, with or without Madison's help.

Chapter Fourteen

Hannah locked her bike up outside the Sleepy Hollow Library and headed inside, determined to find out more about the ghost cat legend. She headed straight for the reference desk, where the librarian was engrossed in a book.

"Excuse me?" Hannah asked hesitantly.

The woman who looked up was the youngest librarian Hannah had ever seen. She also had a nose ring and a pink streak in her dirty-blond hair. *Cool!* Hannah thought. She'd been going to the Tarrytown Library her entire life, and she couldn't ever recall seeing a librarian there who was under fifty.

"Yes, what can I do for you?" the librarian asked.

"I'm looking for information about some old Sleepy Hollow legends," Hannah said. "Uh, for a history project," she added lamely.

"That shouldn't be too hard to find," the librarian replied. "We set up a special section with books about local history and folklore every October. They can't be checked out, but feel free to use them while you're here at the library. Lots of people like to read about ghost legends around Halloween, and this town is famous for those."

Hannah smiled. "Ghost legends sound great," she said.

"They should be right over there." The librarian pointed to a table covered in fake cobwebs. A plastic bat hung above the display of books.

"Perfect, thanks," Hannah said. Then she headed over to the bookshelf. The top shelf was full of fiction, and Hannah saw a few books of short stories by Washington Irving. Below that was a row of history books. There was *Stone Stories: Tombstones Throughout the Ages*, *Popular Legends and Curses*, and an incredibly thick, dusty old book called *Legends of the Hudson Valley*. Hannah pulled that one off the shelf along with a cloud of dust that made her cough.

She carried the book over to one of the wooden desks in the reading area and plunked it down with a loud thud. The man at the desk next to her glanced up and glared. Hannah ducked her head sheepishly and slipped into a chair. Then she flipped the book open and turned to the index.

The first thing she looked up was *ghost cat*, but there was nothing listed. Then she tried *Sleepy Hollow Cemetery*, but all she found were references to Ichabod Crane and the headless horseman. Finally, she tried *haunting*, and discovered a chapter all about ghosts in the Hudson Valley.

Hannah learned that Washington Irving's home in Tarrytown, which was called Sunnyside, had supposedly been haunted when he lived there. She shivered. Her mom loved Sunnyside — they'd just been there together that summer, for an afternoon picnic next to the Hudson River.

Hannah almost laughed at herself for being creeped out. After all, hadn't she herself been *living* in a haunted house for the past two weeks? She continued to skim the chapter, reading about the haunted castle on Bannerman Island and other local spots that were rumored to be stomping grounds for ghosts.

Finally, she came to a section featuring legends of the Sleepy Hollow Cemetery.

One of the lesser-known legends of the Hudson Valley region is the story of Molly Straub of Sleepy Hollow. Born in 1847, Molly was the daughter of a wealthy businessman. Her mother died in childbirth, and Molly lived alone with her father in a large mansion overlooking the Hudson River.

There were no other houses nearby, and Molly was a lonely child without any playmates. She did have a small black cat that she used to dress in doll dresses and bonnets. The cat followed Molly everywhere, and no one in town ever saw her without the cat a few paces behind her. The local townsfolk called the cat Molly's "shadow," and that became the cat's name.

Many of these same villagers were superstitious people, and they thought black cats were terribly bad luck. In particular, the villagers thought Molly's cat was bewitched because it allowed her to dress it in clothing without protesting. The villagers were vocal about their disapproval of Molly's pet.

The house where Molly and her father lived included a small river dock on the property, and Molly's father would occasionally row her out to one of the little islands in the river for a picnic. Molly knew that she was never, ever to take the rowboat out on her own. But on All Hallow's Eve the year Molly turned twelve, she went out in the little boat and never came back. Shadow disappeared on the same day. A week later, Molly's body was found, drowned in the river. No one knew what had happened, but the villagers were certain that the cat had lured Molly to her death. Legend has it that the cat still haunts the Sleepy Hollow Cemetery, where Molly is buried.

Hannah closed the book. She felt weak. It was true — all of it. Paisley's story about the ghost cat matched this one exactly.

Then Hannah gasped. *All Hallow's Eve.* The book said Molly and her cat had disappeared on that day. All Hallow's Eve was Halloween! And Halloween was the very next weekend. Hannah had been so stressed out lately, she had forgotten all about it. And hadn't there been a rowboat in her dream the other night? The dream where Madison had turned into a black cat?

Hannah pushed back her chair and stood up abruptly. She had to get out of the library immediately.

She got another glare and a *"Shhhh!"* from the man next to her, but Hannah barely noticed. She stumbled toward the exit and almost didn't see the young librarian step in front of her as she headed for the door.

"Didn't you forget something?" the woman asked, holding up Hannah's jacket. "It was on the back of your chair."

"Oh!" Hannah exclaimed. "Thank you!"

The librarian handed Hannah the jacket. "I didn't mean to startle you. Is everything okay?" she asked, a concerned look on her face. "Did you find everything you were looking for?"

"No — I mean, yes!" Hannah said hurriedly. "I mean, thanks so much for your help."

Hannah rushed out of the building before the librarian could ask her more questions. She had no idea where she was rushing to, but she needed some time to think. Maybe a long ride on her bike would —

"Hannah?" someone behind her called out. Hannah spun around to see Taylor Walsh hurrying down the steps to the library. "I thought that was you! I called out to you before, but you ran out of the library so quickly you must not have heard me."

Taylor seemed to take in Hannah's wild-eyed look, because suddenly she became alarmed herself.

"Are you okay?" she asked, a worried look on her face. "Did something happen?"

"What? No, I'm fine," Hannah said unconvincingly. "It's just — uh, my dad called to tell me I have to come home right away. I think I'm in trouble or something."

Hannah couldn't believe how good she was getting at these little white lies. They just seemed to keep slipping out lately.

"Oh no!" Taylor said sympathetically. "That stinks. Well, I just wanted to invite you to the Halloween party Ryan and I are throwing next Saturday. I know it's the day after Halloween, but we figured no one would come Friday night because they'd all be out trick-or-treating. It starts at six o'clock. You should totally come. Oh, and bring your friend Paisley. She plays soccer with my friends Alice and Indira, so you can tell her they'll be there, too."

Two weeks ago, Hannah would have been thrilled to be invited to a boy-girl Halloween party. Now she couldn't think of anything except what bad luck and hauntings Halloween might bring. What if something terrible happened to her — or to Madison — that Friday night?

"I, uh, I'll have to ask my dad, but that sounds like fun," Hannah replied. "And I'll ask Paisley, too. I'll let you know."

"Okay, cool," Taylor replied. "See ya!"

Taylor headed back into the library, and Hannah unlocked her bike and headed for home, a million thoughts and fears swarming around in her head. Hannah was certain *something* scary was going to happen on Halloween. The only question was what that something would be.

Chapter Fifteen

On Monday morning, Hannah woke in a daze. The scratching sound seemed to have gotten louder and more insistent the previous night, and she had barely slept. Madison looked just as tired as Hannah felt as the two girls stumbled to the bus stop together. When the bus pulled up, Madison got on and headed straight for her seat next to Alexis. Hannah slipped into the next empty seat she found and immediately fell into a half-sleep.

A second later, she was jolted awake as someone sat down on the bench next to her.

"Hey," Ryan said with a crooked grin. "Sorry to wake you."

Hannah sat up straight and swiped at her mouth with the back of her hand. Had she been drooling?

Please don't let me have been drooling! she thought desperately. *That would be* so *embarrassing, and I already have plenty of other things to worry about.*

"Uh, that's okay," Hannah said. "I was up late last night and didn't sleep well."

"I can see that," Ryan teased. "I just wanted to make sure you knew about the Halloween party Taylor and I are having next weekend. She told me she saw you at the library yesterday and invited you, but I wanted to make sure you were coming."

Hannah thought she might have been imagining it, but Ryan seemed a little nervous. He kept jiggling his leg up and down.

"Yeah, that sounds like fun," Hannah said. She tried to push thoughts of the ghost cat out of her head. A party would be a fun distraction, right? *As long as nothing terrible happens before then*, she thought. She hadn't even remembered Halloween was coming up so soon until Taylor had brought it up. "Do I have to wear a costume?"

"You don't *have* to, but isn't that half the fun?" Ryan replied. "I'm going as a mad scientist. I even have a prop — a beaker full of cola and a bunch of Mentos candies, so I can make the soda bubble over!"

"That sounds awesome," Hannah said. She was impressed. Boys usually didn't put much thought into their Halloween costumes, but Ryan obviously had. And his idea was pretty cool. "I guess I'll have to come up with something fast."

"I'm sure you'll think of something," Ryan said. "There are lots of easy costumes out there. You could wrap yourself in toilet paper and go as a mummy, or you could wear black and put on ears and a tail and go as a cat. Or you could just wear a white sheet and be a ghost!"

Hannah's breath caught in her throat. Why had Ryan mentioned both cats and ghosts? Did he know something, or had it just been a coincidence? There was an awkward silence between them.

"You okay?" Ryan asked gently. "Did I say something weird?"

Hannah shook her head. "No, no, sorry," she said apologetically. "I'm just so tired, I'm a little out of it. Those are great ideas — thanks."

"Sure, anytime," he said. "Oh, and there's one other thing — our band, The Headless Horsemen, is playing at the party. If you wanted to play with us, that would be awesome. I'd rather play bass, so we could really use a guitarist. We only know one song so far, but it's a pretty good one. I can write down the chords for you if you want."

Hannah picked nervously at a patch she'd sewn onto her backpack. "Um, maybe," she said hesitantly. It sounded like so much fun. She wished she had the confidence to just say yes, but she was still scared of a repeat of the great ballet disaster, especially since so many kids from her school would be there. "I guess you could give me the chords so I can try practicing them and see how it goes. Can I let you know for sure later in the week?"

Ryan grinned again, even more broadly this time. "Definitely! Let me write them down now."

He pulled a sheet of paper out of his notebook and began scribbling feverishly with a stubby pencil. As the bus pulled up in front of the school, Ryan handed Hannah the scrawled notes. "Here you go," he said. "If you write down your e-mail address for me, I'll send you an MP3 of the song, too. We're going to get together to practice on Saturday before everyone gets to the party, so if you decide you want to play with us, it would be great if you can come over a little early."

Hannah tore out a sheet of paper from her own notebook and wrote down her e-mail address for

Ryan. "Sounds like a deal," she agreed as she handed him the paper.

When Hannah got to homeroom, Paisley was nowhere to be found. Even though Hannah wasn't supposed to use her cell phone in school, she slipped into the girls' bathroom between her English and bio classes and sent Paisley a quick text:

where r u??? missed u in homeroom!

Hannah didn't get a reply until lunchtime:

ugh! home sick. :(slept all a.m. will call 2nite.

The rest of the day flew by in a sleepy blur. Hannah managed to stay awake in all of her classes, but she felt like a zombie for most of the day. By the time she got home, she was ready to collapse. She did her homework as quickly as possible and was about to climb into bed when her cell phone chimed. It was a text from Paisley:

can u skype? just woke up from 3rd nap of the day!

sure. just give me a sec.

Hannah logged on and her friend's face filled the computer screen. Paisley looked pretty miserable — her cheeks were flushed and her eyes were glassy.

"How are you feeling?" Hannah asked. "Don't take this the wrong way, but you look, well, you look like you're sick."

"Uhhh, I know!" Paisley said. "I slept most of the day."

"Sorry," Hannah said sympathetically. "If it makes you feel better, you didn't miss anything exciting in homeroom this morning. Oh, but I saw Taylor Walsh at the library yesterday, and she invited both of us to her Halloween party on Saturday. Well, her and her brother Ryan's party."

Hannah felt her cheeks get hotter when she said Ryan's name.

"Are you blushing?" Paisley teased. "Oh my gosh! You like him! You totally have a crush on Ryan Walsh!"

"No, I do not," Hannah said halfheartedly. She wanted to deny it, but she suddenly realized it was true. She *did* like Ryan. In fact, hanging out with him had been one of the only good things that had happened to her lately. She sighed. Then she smiled. "Okay, maybe I do. But just a little bit!"

"Eeeeek!" Paisley shrieked. "He's really cute. And nice. I approve one hundred percent."

Hannah blushed again. It felt good to talk about boys with her friend. For a few minutes, she had forgotten all about the ghost cat. But then suddenly, she heard the scratching sound.

Scratch, scratch, scratch.

Hannah stopped smiling immediately, and her face paled. The mild dread she had been feeling in the pit of her stomach since her trip to the library intensified. She glanced behind her, but of course there was nothing there.

"Hannah?" Paisley asked. "You okay?"

"Um, yeah, I'm fine," Hannah said a little too quickly. Paisley looked at her suspiciously. Again, Hannah considered confessing everything to her friend. Paisley would believe her, right? She wouldn't think Hannah was making it all up, would she? Hannah honestly didn't know how Paisley would respond, but she knew if Paisley didn't believe her, it could be the end of their friendship. Things had been rocky enough since their fight, and Hannah realized that wasn't a risk she was willing to take.

"I — um, I'm just still sad about Icky," Hannah told Paisley. *At least that's not a lie*, she thought.

"Still no word?" Paisley replied, her brow wrinkled in concern. "I've been keeping an eye out for him around here, you know. I keep hoping I'll find him hiding in our bushes when I take out the trash."

Hannah sighed. It was nice to know that her friend had been thinking of Icky and looking for him, too. "Thanks, Pais," she said softly. "You're a great friend."

Suddenly, Paisley was overcome by a fit of coughing. When she finally stopped, she looked exhausted from the effort.

"I think I'd better go," she said with a smile. "Time for some cough medicine and more sleep."

"Yeah, I should go to sleep, too," Hannah replied, even though she doubted she would be able to sleep much that night. Now in addition to worrying about the ghost cat, she was thinking about Icky, too. Hannah had a feeling it was going to be a very long night.

As the week dragged on and Halloween approached, Hannah slept less and less. The scratching sound intensified at night, but was gone each morning, and nothing else suspicious happened. Hannah spent a lot of time practicing her guitar along with the MP3 Ryan had sent and researching curses and ghosts online. For every story she read about a menacing spirit, there was at least one story about a benevolent and kind ghost who was only haunting someone out of boredom or for fun.

Seriously? Hannah thought. *Ghosts haunt people for fun?* She vowed that should she ever become a ghost in her own afterlife, she would never, *ever* haunt someone just because she found it entertaining.

The only time Hannah seemed to be able to relax enough to think things over was when she was playing her guitar. By Wednesday night, she had mastered The Headless Horsemen's one and only song, "Skeleton Riot."

As she strummed easily through the chords, Hannah thought about the ghost cat. She desperately wanted to believe the ghost was the good kind of spirit — after all, it was a cat, and she loved cats. But how would she ever know for sure? The more Hannah thought about it, the more confused she was about everything. If the ghost *wasn't* trying to do her harm, then what was it after? Could the haunting have something to do with Icky's disappearance? If not, then what in the world would the ghost of an old cat want from Hannah?

She didn't have a clue.

And as Hannah packed her guitar in its case on Wednesday night, just two days before Halloween, she had a feeling she was going to have to wait until Friday to find out.

Chapter Sixteen

Hannah woke on Thursday feeling as confused as ever about the ghost. She also hadn't made any progress on her plans for a Halloween costume *or* decided whether or not she was going to play with The Headless Horsemen. And, of course, Icky was still missing. Her stomach was a bundle of knotted nerves.

As she brushed her teeth and got ready for school, she made a silent vow to herself. By the end of the day, she was determined to have at least two of those issues resolved — she had to let Ryan know whether she was going to play with The Headless Horsemen, and she had to find something to wear to the party.

Surprisingly, the costume issue resolved itself over breakfast. Hannah walked into the kitchen to find Madison and Allison in the middle of an argument.

"Mom, I *told* you I already had a costume," Madison snapped at Allison through a mouthful of cereal. "Alexis, Katie, and I got vintage twenties-style dresses at the thrift store, and we're going to be flappers."

Allison sighed. She picked up a shopping bag and pulled out a black vest with a skull-and-crossbones patch on it and a red-and-black striped skirt. Hannah also caught a glimpse of a glittery black eye patch.

"But this pirate costume is so *adorable*!" Allison insisted. "And it was such a great deal. When I saw it on the sale rack, I couldn't resist. Now it's going to go to waste."

"Ugh, a pirate?" Madison countered, her voice dripping with disdain. "Seriously, Mom, no girl wants to be a pirate. It's so *not* cute. There was totally a reason it was on sale."

"I'll wear it," Hannah said simply. Madison and Allison both looked at her in surprise.

"What?" Hannah asked with a shrug. "I need a costume for Halloween, and I think it's cute. The eye patch is covered in black sequins."

Madison snorted into her cereal. "Figures," she muttered under her breath.

Hannah glared at her in reply.

"What was that?" Allison asked her daughter sharply. For the first time, she seemed aware of the tension between the two girls.

"Nothing," Madison said sweetly. "I just had a little tickle in my throat."

Hannah reached out to take the costume from Allison. "Thanks," she said.

"No problem," Allison replied. She still seemed surprised, but she smiled warmly at Hannah. "I'm glad someone will get some use out of it."

Hannah really did like the costume, especially the skull-and-crossbones patch, which was accessorized with red gemstones. And it seemed like the kind of costume The Headless Horsemen would approve of, too, even if she hadn't yet decided whether she was going to join their band.

One problem down, two to go, Hannah thought as she grabbed a cereal bar and ran upstairs to get her backpack, guitar, and coat before heading outside to wait for the bus.

As she stepped out the front door, Hannah practically slammed into Madison, who was standing motionless in the middle of the porch. She was staring at the ground, her face ashen.

"What's wrong?" Hannah asked as she glanced down. There on the step in front of them was a mangled, bloody dead animal. Hannah gasped.

"Wh-wh-what is it?" Madison whispered. She sounded terrified.

Hannah wanted to run screaming into the house, but like Madison, fear had rooted her in place on the porch. She felt dread return to the pit of her stomach as she gathered up all of her courage and leaned over to get a closer look.

Relief flooded through Hannah in a wave that made her weak in the knees. Even though there was nothing funny about the situation, she let out a little laugh.

"It's not a real animal — it's a stuffed toy," Hannah told Madison as she crouched down to examine the gray ball of fake fur. "See? The red stuff isn't blood either — it's paint or something."

"It's Mr. Mouse," Madison said softly, the expression on her face a mixture of fear and nostalgia.

"Mr. Mouse?" Hannah asked. "Who's that?"

"He was my favorite toy when I was little — a stuffed gray mouse. My mom kept him stored in a box of my old baby things in the garage. . . ."

She trailed off. Hannah realized what she was thinking. The mouse had been in the garage the other day when her dad had fallen off the ladder and spilled the paint because of the ghost cat. And now the toy was covered in paint and looked like it had been attacked by some sort of animal. There was only one way it could have gotten to the porch steps — the ghost cat.

Suddenly, Madison sprang into action. She grabbed the toy and marched down the walkway toward the garbage cans that were lined up neatly at the curb. Then she yanked the lid off one of the cans and threw the toy in before slamming the lid down again. Madison wiped her palms on her jeans and walked purposefully toward the bus stop.

Hannah followed closely behind her, a million thoughts racing through her head. What did the mangled toy mean? Was it some sort of sign? Or had the ghost cat just found a fun toy to play with? Hannah glanced at Madison and noticed that she was furiously wiping away tears.

"Madison, we need to talk about this," Hannah said desperately. "We have to figure out why all of this stuff keeps happening. I did some research at the library this weekend, and there's something you should know."

Madison remained silent as Hannah told her the complete story of Molly Straub and her cat, Shadow. Hannah explained that she was worried something terrible might happen on Halloween since that was the night when Molly Straub had drowned.

By the time Hannah finished, the bus was rounding the corner. "Well, what do you think?" Hannah asked. "Don't you think we need to figure out why we're being haunted?"

"If anyone's being haunted, it's you," Madison replied tersely. The bus squealed to a stop and the doors opened. "And I'm not talking about this anymore," Madison hissed under her breath as she boarded the bus.

Hannah slid into an empty seat and propped her backpack and guitar case next to her. She sighed heavily. She couldn't believe how ridiculous and selfish Madison was being. *How can she care so much about being popular that she doesn't even want to figure out what the ghost wants?* Hannah thought. She punched the back of the bus seat in frustration just as Ryan slid into the seat next to her.

"Whoa," he joked. "Rough morning?"

"You could say that," Hannah replied glumly.

"What happened?" Ryan asked.

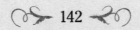

Hannah sighed. "It's a long story."

Ryan shrugged. "I've got an entire bus ride," he said. "And there's lunch, too."

Hannah hesitated. Had Ryan just asked her to eat lunch with him? Should she tell him what was going on? Madison hadn't been any help so far, Hannah's dad wouldn't believe her even if she had told him the whole story, and Hannah was too afraid of what Paisley might think to tell her what had been happening lately. But maybe telling someone else would lead to some answers. And at this point, she was feeling desperate. Halloween was the next day, and she needed to do something before then.

Hannah took a deep breath and decided to go for it.

She leaned toward Ryan and lowered her voice until it was just a whisper.

"Do you believe in ghosts?"

Chapter Seventeen

There was a long pause before Ryan replied. Hannah realized she was holding her breath. Was he going to laugh at her?

"Um, yeah, who doesn't?" Ryan finally replied, his eyes wide. "There's a reason ghost stories exist, right? It's not like people had a lot of free time on their hands in olden times, you know? They had a lot of farm work and cooking and stuff to do. So if they were telling stories about ghosts and hauntings, there must have been a reason why."

Hannah had never really thought of it that way before. "Well, it also could have been because they didn't have TVs and movies for entertainment," she said with a shrug.

Ryan laughed. "Or that," he agreed. "So what about ghosts?"

Hannah couldn't believe she'd finally found someone to confide in. But of course, by then, the bus was already pulling up in front of the school.

"I'll tell you everything at lunch, okay?" Hannah replied.

"That's a real cliffhanger!" Ryan teased. Then, seeing the look on Hannah's face, he became serious. "Something tells me it's one heck of a story."

"Yeah, you could say that," Hannah agreed, a grim look on her face. "See you at lunch."

"See ya!" Ryan replied, flashing Hannah a smile and a wave before dashing off to his homeroom.

The entire morning seemed to crawl by. Hannah couldn't wait until lunch so she could talk to Ryan, but every class seemed twice as long as usual. When Hannah got to math class, she was almost relieved that there was a pop quiz because it forced her to focus on something other than the clock.

Finally, the bell rang at the end of Hannah's last class before lunch. She hurried to the cafeteria as quickly as she could without sprinting through the halls. Ryan was already there, and he had saved her a seat. He seemed as happy to see Hannah as she was to see him. Hannah felt an unexpected warmth fill her chest as he smiled at her and gestured to the empty seat.

"Okay," he said urgently as soon as she sat down. "Spill it."

Hannah told him everything — from the scratching sound she heard at night to the black cat she followed into the cemetery, to the overflowing bathtub, to her suspicions that Madison knew something was up but didn't want to admit it.

Ryan listened so closely to the entire story that both his and Hannah's grilled cheese sandwiches sat completely untouched. By the time Hannah picked up her sandwich and took a bite, it was ice-cold.

"Whew," Ryan whistled softly. He took a bite of his sandwich as well. "That's really intense."

Hannah nodded. As scared as she still was about everything, she suddenly felt a million times lighter. For the past few weeks, she had felt an enormous weight on her shoulders, not unlike the time a few years ago at the beach when she had insisted that Paisley bury her up to her chin in the sand. Now she felt as though she had broken through the mound of sand and was finally free to splash in the waves again.

"It feels better just to talk to someone about it," Hannah admitted, amazed at how true it was. "But I'm still not sure what to do. I guess I'll just have to wait and see what happens."

Ryan had a thoughtful look on his face. "I suppose you *could* just wait and see," he agreed somewhat reluctantly. He leaned forward eagerly, his eyes bright with excitement. "Or you could take matters into your own hands."

"What do you mean?" asked Hannah, alarmed. "It's not like I'm some sort of ghostbuster or something."

"No, but I've heard there are some things you can do to ward off ghosts," he continued enthusiastically. "You know how vampires hate garlic? Well, I'm sure there's some stuff ghosts hate, too. I have computer class this afternoon and we've had a sub all week. I'll bet I can do some research to find out what kinds of things ghosts are afraid of."

"That would be great," Hannah said. She was so tired of being scared all the time that trying a few superstitious tricks didn't seem like a bad idea. If nothing worked, she would be no worse off than she was now.

"I'll write down whatever I find out and I'll give it to you when I see you before my guitar lesson tonight," Ryan said. "And speaking of guitar, what do you think about the party on Saturday? Are you going to play with us?"

For a second, the fear moved in and threatened to take over, but something made Hannah stop herself from saying no. If she could handle a ghost, she could handle a little stage fright. She took a deep breath.

"Okay, I'll do it," Hannah said. She smiled. Just saying the words aloud made her feel more confident that she truly *could* do it. Even if she froze for a second onstage, she would get over it. She knew she could.

"Great!" Ryan said as the bell rang for the end of lunch. "I'll see you later at Mr. G.'s."

Hannah's guitar lesson that afternoon was the best one she'd ever had. All of the time she'd spent practicing "Skeleton Riot" that week had really paid off.

"Wow, Hannah," Mr. G. gushed. "That sounded fantastic!"

"Thanks," Hannah replied. "I've been feeling a lot more confident about my playing lately."

"Does that mean you're ready to try playing in my recital?" Mr. G. asked.

Hannah had forgotten all about the recital. But now that she had agreed to play with The Headless Horsemen, it seemed silly not to agree to the recital, too.

"Can I choose the song?" Hannah asked hesitantly.

"Yes, as long as I approve it," Mr. G. said.

"Okay, I'll do it," Hannah said for the second time that day.

"Fantastic!" Mr. G. exclaimed. "In that case, you're free to go a bit early. I'm sure you're excited to get home to prepare for Halloween tomorrow."

Hannah's smile dissolved. In her excitement over her lunch with Ryan and her guitar lesson, she had completely forgotten about the following day. "Right, Halloween," she said tersely.

Mr. G. looked perplexed, but there was no way Hannah could explain everything to him. Instead, she packed up as quickly as she could and headed out into the waiting room.

Luckily, Ryan was there early, and he handed Hannah a piece of paper that had been folded into an origami star.

"Good luck!" he told Hannah encouragingly before he went into the studio for his lesson.

"Thanks," she whispered as she took the star and slipped it into her pocket. "See you in school tomorrow." Then she headed outside to wait for her dad to pick her up.

As soon as Hannah got home, she unwrapped the star to read Ryan's note.

Hannah —

Okay, here's what I found out. There are a few things you can do to keep a ghost away:

1. Put salt in your pocket. I don't know how much this will help, but it can't hurt. The worst thing is you'll have salty jeans.

2. Mint keeps bad spirits away. I guess this means you should eat a lot of Altoids or peppermints?

3. Burning a bunch of pine needles and sage is supposed to clear your home of ghosts and bad luck. This doesn't sound like a good idea to me, though,

because it involves open flames, and I got in big trouble for something like that over the summer (don't ask).

4. Charms. I don't think these are the lucky cereal kind — I think they're more like poems. If you write one that says something about keeping the ghost cat away and say it over and over again, that might work. Oh, and it should rhyme. You can also write it on a piece of paper and wear it in something around your neck to bring good fortune.

I guess that's it. Good luck with the ghost, and see you in school tomorrow.

Your friend,
Ryan

Hannah wondered what it meant that Ryan had signed the note "your friend." Was he trying to tell her that he only liked her as a friend? Or did it mean something else? Hannah wasn't sure how she would have signed a note to him, but she thought she probably would have just written her name. She sighed. As if she didn't have enough to worry about!

After dinner that night, Hannah managed to sneak the saltshaker and some mint tea bags upstairs to her room. First she cut open the tea bags and sprinkled the leaves across each windowsill. Then she put the salt in the pockets of her pajama pants. She felt silly as she sprinkled the tea and salt on her things, but she also felt strangely confident and brave. For the first time, Hannah felt like she was taking charge of the ghost situation and doing something to try to prevent something bad from happening. She was finally standing up for herself, and it felt good, even if she *was* just standing up to a ghost.

Since she didn't have any sage or pine needles, Hannah skipped that one. She also agreed with Ryan that burning stuff probably wasn't the best idea. Finally, there was the charm. Hannah pulled out a piece of paper and tried to come up with something to recite, but nothing came to her. After thirty minutes of staring at the blank sheet of paper, she gave up and climbed into bed.

She crossed her fingers that the salt and mint alone would do the trick.

Chapter Eighteen

On Friday morning, Hannah woke up to find that she had slept through the entire night without waking up once. It had worked! The salt and mint tea had kept the ghost cat away! There had been no scratching sound to wake her. Hannah couldn't believe her good luck. Now all she had to do was get through Halloween, and maybe, just maybe, this entire haunting ordeal would be behind her.

Hannah pulled on her favorite jeans, T-shirt, and hooded cardigan. Even though it was Halloween, no one was allowed to wear costumes to school because the teachers thought it was too distracting.

When Hannah got to homeroom, she was thrilled to see Paisley was back.

"Hey!" Hannah said as she slid into her seat. "Welcome back. Feeling better?"

Paisley smiled. "Mostly," she said. "My mom told me if I was feeling well enough to consider playing in my soccer game tomorrow and going to Taylor and Ryan's party, I was well enough to go to school. So here I am."

"Well, I'm glad you're back," Hannah said. "And I'm glad you're going to come to the party tomorrow, too."

"Ms. Lingren! Ms. Malloy!" their homeroom teacher, Mr. Jaffe, barked at them. "Do you mind if I continue to take attendance?"

"Sorry, Mr. Jaffe," Hannah squeaked. There was only one rule about talking in homeroom — it wasn't allowed during attendance. As soon as Mr. Jaffe had finished the roll call, Hannah turned back to talk to Paisley about the party. But Paisley was engrossed in her vocabulary notebook.

"Sorry, Hannah," Paisley said apologetically. "I have to study these vocab words. I've got a ton of catching up to do. Can we talk more tonight? I'll be home — that's another condition my mom placed on me."

"Okay," Hannah agreed. "We can talk later."

Paisley smiled. "Thanks. You're the best."

For the rest of the morning, whenever a little wave of worry swept over Hannah, she patted her jeans pocket, which she had filled with salt that morning before school. She felt silly about the whole thing, but it *did* make her feel better.

At lunch, Ryan and Taylor invited Hannah to sit at their table with a bunch of their friends.

"This is Hannah," Taylor told the table. "She's joining our band. You can hear her play guitar tomorrow at our Halloween party!"

Hannah felt herself freeze up just looking at the sea of faces at the lunch table, and she wasn't even on a stage *or* holding her guitar! *Just breathe*, she reminded herself. *Just relax and take a deep breath. They'll all be wearing costumes tomorrow, so you'll hardly recognize them.*

Hannah forced herself to smile at everyone before she sat down.

"Hi," a few of the kids at the table said before returning to their lunches and conversations.

Ryan sat down next to Hannah.

"Hey," he whispered. "How did it go last night? Did you try the mints and salt?"

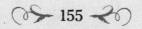

Hannah patted her pocket and nodded. "Yup, I've got the salt right here," she whispered back as she ate a bite of her salad. "And the mint seemed to help, too — I didn't hear anything last night! Maybe the worst of it is over."

A few hours later, Hannah was sitting in her bedroom, hoping she had been right. Was the worst of it over? Would she make it through Halloween unscathed, or would the ghost cat strike again? There was only one way to find out — she had to wait.

Hannah passed the time by practicing her guitar and chatting online with Paisley about the party the next day. She and Paisley had decided that they were a little too old to trick-or-treat this year, even though Hannah knew plenty of kids in her class would be out around the neighborhood. Plus, Hannah figured she'd be too jumpy to enjoy the trick-or-treating, anyway.

So instead, Hannah told Paisley all about the band and about the song she had been practicing with them. She still didn't have the courage to tell her friend about the ghost, though. Even though Ryan had believed her, Hannah still worried that Paisley might not. And where would Hannah be without her best friend? She wasn't sure she wanted to find out.

By eight o'clock, the few trick-or-treaters who

had braved the house next to the cemetery had come and gone, and Hannah was in her room. There was a soft knock on her door. Hannah was surprised to find Madison standing on the other side. Their parents had gone out to an adults-only Halloween party, and they weren't going to be back until after midnight, so she and Madison were home alone.

Madison looked annoyed, but she also looked anxious.

"You want to watch a movie in my room?" she asked in a bored tone. "*I'm* fine by myself, but I thought *you* might want some company since you seemed so worried about there being a ghost in the house."

Madison laughed. Hannah was pretty sure she was trying to sound cool, but instead she just sounded really scared and nervous. Hannah wasn't sure how to respond. She didn't exactly want to be alone either, but Madison certainly wasn't at the top of the list of people Hannah wanted to hang out with.

"Um, sure," Hannah agreed reluctantly. "A movie sounds good. What do you want to watch?"

Madison's shoulders relaxed and she seemed relieved. Hannah followed her into her bedroom, which was so pink it hurt Hannah's eyes. Madison picked a romantic comedy and Hannah didn't argue —

there was no way she wanted to watch a serious or scary movie tonight.

Neither of them talked during the movie, but that was also fine with Hannah. She wasn't sure what she would have said, anyway. When the credits began to roll, it was just after ten o'clock, and Hannah yawned loudly.

"Well, uh, thanks for the movie," Hannah said awkwardly. "I should probably go to bed. See you in the morning."

"Fine," Madison snapped.

Back to her usual nasty self, Hannah thought as she returned to her own room and climbed into bed. Almost as soon as her head hit the pillow she was fast asleep.

Scratch, scratch, scratch.

Hannah jolted awake at the sound. She glanced at her clock and saw that it was almost midnight. The scratching was louder than ever, and it sounded like it was right under her window. And then Hannah heard something else — a plaintive meow.

She jumped out of bed and dashed to the window. She peered out and saw the dark shape of a cat illuminated by the moonlight. The cat meowed again, more loudly this time.

"Shoo!" Hannah called out. "Go away!"

The cat turned and took a few steps away from the house. Hannah gasped. In the moonlight, she could see a small patch of white on the tip of the tail. It was Icky!

"Icky!" Hannah called out desperately. "Wait! I'm coming!"

Hannah grabbed a sweatshirt from the back of her desk chair and pulled it on over her pajamas. Then she rummaged frantically in her closet until she found her big camping flashlight. She couldn't believe Icky had found her after all these weeks . . . it was incredible!

She ran down the stairs and quickly peeked out the front window to see if her dad was home yet, but the driveway was empty. *I guess I'll have to go after Icky by myself*, Hannah thought. She wasn't thrilled about heading outside alone so late at night, but there was also no way she was letting Icky get away again. Hannah hurried through the kitchen and out the back door. When she got outside, though, she didn't see Icky anywhere.

"Icky?" she called out. "Where are you, boy? Come on out."

A second later, she saw a movement toward the

back of the yard, near the cemetery gate. Hannah's heart quickened. *Not the cemetery!* she thought. *Please, Icky, please, please, please don't make me follow you into the cemetery on Halloween night!*

For a second, Hannah was frozen in place, terrified. If she didn't follow Icky, he might never return, and she didn't think she could bear that. But on the other hand, following him meant going into the cemetery in the dark — on Halloween. It only took Hannah a second to make up her mind. She took a deep breath and hurried after her cat.

Hannah paused when she reached the cemetery gate. Her heart was clamoring against her chest, but she forced herself to take a few deep, calming breaths. Then she gathered her courage and lifted her hand to the latch. Suddenly, there was a rustling sound behind her.

Hannah whirled around. As she turned, a light caught her full in the face, temporarily blinding her.

"Ahhhh!" Hannah yelped, her hands shielding her eyes. "Who is it? Who's there?"

The light shifted and Hannah saw that it was Madison, holding a flashlight of her own. She was trembling. "It's just me," she squeaked softly. She looked absolutely terrified. "Sorry, I didn't mean to shine the light right in your face. I just panicked."

Hannah was astounded. "What are you doing out here?" she asked Madison. She had no idea why Madison would have followed her, not after all of her efforts to keep Hannah away from the cemetery.

"I heard the scratching and the meowing," Madison admitted softly. "You were right — I've heard it all along, I just didn't want to believe it."

Hannah didn't know what to say.

"I saw you head out into the backyard, and I was so scared!" Madison continued. "I mean, I'm not thrilled that I have to share my bathroom, but I don't want you to, like, die or something. What if there really is a ghost? I could never forgive myself if something terrible happened to you."

Hannah was shocked. "Thanks," she said, still astounded by Madison's change of heart. "But I'm not following a ghost — I'm following my cat, Icky. I saw him under my window, and I know it was definitely him. The cat was black with a white patch on his tail. That's exactly what Icky looks like."

Madison was trembling so much her flashlight was shaking. Hannah couldn't tell if it was because she was cold or afraid.

"Well, I'm still coming," Madison said stubbornly.

"Then let's go," Hannah said with a nod toward the gate. She pushed it open with a loud *creak*, and Madison followed her hesitantly into the cemetery.

"Icky?" Hannah called. "Where are you?"

The girls heard a loud *meow* just a few feet ahead of them. Madison jumped, startled, but she quickly regained her composure. The girls moved purposefully toward the sound.

Hannah was trying her best not to think of the dark shadows the trees were casting all around her as she and Madison moved deeper and deeper into the cemetery. They were surrounded by ancient, crumbling tombstones, and Hannah could only see a foot or so in front of her because that was as far as the beam of her flashlight reached. Suddenly, the light flickered. In an instant, the bulb darkened considerably.

Madison gasped. "Did you bring extra batteries?" she whispered.

Hannah shook her head. She tried to think back to the last time she had gone camping and put fresh batteries in her flashlight, but she couldn't remember. It had been at least a year. The light flickered again, and Hannah grabbed Madison's arm.

"I guess it's a good thing you brought your own flashlight," she joked with a nervous laugh.

"That's not funny," Madison snapped back, annoyed. "For someone who sneaks into graveyards at night, you're not very prepared."

"Well, it's not like I do this on a regular basis," Hannah replied sharply. She took another step forward and stumbled on something. "Ouch!"

Madison aimed her flashlight at Hannah's foot as Hannah rubbed her sore toe. Looking up, Hannah realized that they were standing right in front of a huge mausoleum and gasped.

"I — I've seen this before," she said hoarsely, her voice choked with fear. "It was in a dream I had."

Madison paled. "Hannah, let's get out of here," she said suddenly, a note of hysteria creeping into her voice. "This place is really giving me the creeps. We can come find Icky in the morning. I'm sure he'll still be here —"

Scratch, scratch, scratch.

The girls clutched each other and screamed. The sound had come from *inside the mausoleum*. Hannah's stomach lurched. She thought she was going to be sick.

"This is exactly how it happened in my dream," she whispered. She glanced up at the tomb and saw that there was one word carved into the stone above the door.

STRAUB

The bell at the top of the cemetery's ancient clock tower began to toll for midnight.

"Hannah, let's go!" Madison started to pull Hannah desperately back toward the backyard and the house as the bell chimed.

A wave of courage swept over Hannah, and she shook off Madison's arm.

"No," Hannah said. Her voice wavered a bit, and she clenched her jaw stubbornly. "NO," she repeated more confidently. "I'm getting to the bottom of this tonight. No more hauntings and no more ghosts. I don't want to live in fear anymore. And it might be Icky trapped inside that tomb!"

Before she could reconsider what she was about to do, Hannah stepped forward and grabbed the cold, metal door handle.

With a tug, she slowly pulled it open. As she did, the clock chimed for a twelfth time and then fell silent.

Chapter Nineteen

There was a rush of cold air from inside the tomb. Hannah and Madison waited, collectively holding their breath to see what would happen next.

Out of the corner of her eye, Hannah saw a black shadow slip inside the tomb. She glanced at Madison to see if she had noticed, but Madison's eyes were glazed over in terror.

There was a rustling sound inside the tomb. Even though Hannah was no longer holding on to the handle, the door creaked open even wider. Hannah gasped and stumbled backward, bumping into Madison and grabbing her arm.

Both girls watched in horror as a shimmery, white ghost stepped out of the tomb. Hannah felt as though the wind had been knocked out of her. She couldn't move, and she couldn't breathe. Her eyes widened as she took in the ghost, a girl about her own age, wearing an old-fashioned dress. She wore her hair in braids tied with pink ribbons.

Madison's teeth were chattering so loudly, Hannah was sure she was going to wake every ghost in the cemetery. And Madison was clutching Hannah's arm so tightly, Hannah was losing feeling in her right hand.

The ghost smiled. "Do not be afraid," she said softly.

Hannah glanced down to see that the girl was holding a small black cat in her arms. The cat was wearing a pink ribbon around its neck that matched the girl's hair bows. Hannah almost laughed, the bow looked so ridiculous. The cat was purring loudly and was clearly not Icky — there was a splash of white on its tail, but all four paws were a sleek, smooth black.

"I am sorry if I frightened you," the ghost continued in a soft, sweet voice. "I do not mean to harm you. I want to thank you so much for opening my tomb. You let my Shadow back inside, and I am forever grateful to you both."

Madison glanced at Hannah in surprise.

"See?" Hannah whispered to Madison. "I told you what I read at the library. This must be Molly!"

The ghost nodded politely at the girls. Then she began to tell her story.

"My name is Molly Straub. I've been living inside this tomb for a very long time, trapped between this world and the next," she explained. "I have been unable to move on without my dear cat, Shadow. He has been haunting this cemetery for more than a hundred years, trying to find a way into my tomb so that we could be reunited."

She sighed softly. "I know all about the terrible stories people told after I drowned," she continued. "The people in this town never liked Shadow. They thought he was the reason I died, but that is not the truth. I was a spoiled girl who always had to get my own way. I wanted to go for a picnic, but Father was too busy to go with me. I was forbidden to take my little rowboat out on the river alone, but I was so angry with Father that I did anyway. Usually, Shadow came out in the boat with me, but I left in such an angry rush, he was left behind on the shore."

Hannah and Madison listened to the girl, their eyes wide.

"It was a lovely, warm day, but as soon as I rowed out to the middle of the river, the wind changed. Dark storm clouds blew in, and it began to rain. I was so far from the shore, and the boat began to rock back and forth violently. The entire time, I could see Shadow pacing on the riverbank, and I could hear him meowing to me. Then a huge wave washed over the boat, and it tipped over. I tried to swim to the shore, but I couldn't do it — the waves were too big, and my dress weighed me down. Through the rain, I could see Shadow trying to swim out to reach me, but then everything went black."

Hannah glanced at Madison and saw that she was wiping away tears.

"All Shadow wanted was to get back to me," Molly explained simply. "But I couldn't open the door to the tomb from the inside — I was trapped in there alone. The door had to be opened from the outside by another child. So, thank you both. Now Shadow and I can rest in peace together . . . forever."

"But what about my cat, Icky?" Hannah asked softly. "I thought I was following him out here tonight. Have you seen him?"

Molly shook her head. "No, I haven't. But I hope you find your cat. Thanks to you, I have finally found mine. I will never forget what you both did for me."

With that, Molly stepped back into the tomb.

Shadow gave one last *meow* before the door to the tomb closed with a gentle *click*.

Hannah turned to Madison, who was still looking about as pale as Molly had been.

"Did that really just happen?" Madison asked, incredulous. "Was that a real ghost?"

Hannah nodded silently. "Yeah," she whispered. "I think it was."

Madison breathed a sigh of relief. "We'd better get home before our parents," she reminded Hannah.

"Yeah, let's go," Hannah replied. She felt an odd combination of relief and disappointment. While she was glad the ghost mystery had been solved, she was upset that she had been so close to finding Icky and yet he had somehow slipped away again.

She followed the beam of Madison's flashlight as they walked back toward the house. When the cemetery gate was just a few steps away, Hannah suddenly heard a soft *meow*.

She glanced at Madison, and it was clear she had heard it, too. Madison rolled her eyes. She no longer seemed scared — now she was just annoyed.

"I thought we were done with this ghost cat," she said with a sigh. But when Hannah turned to follow the meowing sound, Madison followed without arguing.

Hannah headed toward the arbor with the stone bench, where the sound had come from. As she moved closer, she heard it again. Hannah pulled back the branches of the shrubs next to the arbor and stepped forward. Madison shined the light on the stone bench.

"Icky!" Hannah shouted. He was curled up on a soft blanket. Hannah scooped the cat and the blanket up and hugged Icky close. "I finally found you! What are you doing all the way over here?"

Icky just purred loudly in reply. Hannah glanced down at the blanket and realized it was the one she had lost in the cemetery the previous week.

Madison smiled and reached out to pet Icky on the head.

"So this is your cat?" she asked. "He's kind of cute, for a cat. I'm more of a dog person myself."

"Figures," Hannah replied as the girls headed for home. To her surprise, Madison laughed at the jab.

"Thanks for coming with me, Madison," Hannah said. "That was really, um, nice."

Madison seemed flustered by the compliment.

"Yeah, well, sorry for being kind of mean to you," she said grudgingly. "I guess I could have been a little nicer."

Hannah couldn't believe it. Madison Van Meter was apologizing to her? It was pretty amazing. She wondered how long it would last. Could it be that they had some sort of truce now?

"You were pretty brave, going out into the cemetery alone and opening Molly's tomb and all that," Madison continued. "I never would have even gone out there if you hadn't gone first."

"Thanks." Hannah blushed. She hadn't felt brave — it had just been something she needed to do.

The girls snuck back into the kitchen through the back door. Hannah fed Icky a can of tuna fish while Madison checked the driveway. Luckily, their parents were still out.

"Well, I guess I'll see you in the morning," Madison said.

"Good night," Hannah replied. She waited for Icky to finish his tuna before she scooped him up and headed upstairs to bed.

Hannah slipped under the covers, and Icky curled up right next to her. She couldn't remember the last time she had been this happy. As she stroked Icky's soft fur, Hannah drifted off into a deep, dreamless sleep.

Chapter Twenty

The next morning, Hannah woke to the smell of blueberry pancakes. She rushed downstairs to find her dad wearing his "I play banjo better than I cook" apron. She always laughed when she saw the apron, because it was true. Also, her dad wasn't a very good banjo player.

"Good morning!" she said happily.

"Wow, someone's in a good mood today," her dad said as he handed her a plate full of pancakes.

"Thanks," Hannah said as she accepted the plate and sat down. Icky brushed up against her legs under the table.

"You'll never guess what the cat dragged in last night," she joked.

Her dad raised an eyebrow. "I have no idea."

 172

"Well, I guess it's more what *I* dragged in — Icky!" Hannah couldn't hide her smile. She picked him up and held him so her dad could see him.

"Well, I'll be," her dad said, a look of wonder on his face. "How on earth did he make it all the way across town? And how did he know where you were?"

Hannah shrugged innocently. "I have no idea," she said. "I just heard a meowing sound outside my window last night, and there he was. So I ran downstairs to let him in. Crazy, huh?"

"Will wonders never cease?" her dad muttered, mostly to himself. "That's great news, and I have even more. The renovations are officially complete!"

"Wow," Hannah replied. "That's great." She didn't care all that much about the renovations, but her dad seemed excited about it.

"I know," he agreed. "It means I have my weekends back. Speaking of, I'm free for a hike today if you like. What do you say? The Blue Ridge trail at noon?"

Hannah was startled. It had been so long since she and her dad had spent any time together she thought it might never happen again. But as much as she wanted to go hiking with him, she had to get to Ryan and Taylor's house before the party to practice.

As soon as she thought of the party, she realized she had never asked her dad for permission to go.

"A hike sounds fun, Dad, but I can't today," Hannah explained. "My friend Taylor and her brother, Ryan, invited me to a Halloween party tonight. And I'm playing guitar in their band, The Headless Horsemen, so I have to go over there early to practice."

Her dad looked impressed. "A band, eh? Well, that's great. I can give you a ride to the party if you like."

"Thanks," Hannah said. "Maybe we can go for a hike tomorrow if the weather's nice."

"It's a deal," her dad replied.

Later that afternoon, Hannah was in her room getting ready. Madison and her friends were going to a party that night at Katie's cousin's place, so Madison was at Katie's getting her flapper costume together. Hannah was thrilled to have the bathroom all to herself.

She put on a black long-sleeved T-shirt and sparkly red tights. Then she added the pirate vest, the red-and-black striped skirt, and her black boots. In addition to the sequin-covered eye patch, the costume came with a glittery silver sword in a rhinestone-studded sheath. Hannah strapped it around her waist and put on the eye patch.

As soon as Hannah's dad dropped her off at Ryan and Taylor's, her anxiety about performing came flooding back. But then Hannah remembered the previous night, and how Madison had told her how brave she had been. If she could follow a ghost cat into a cemetery at midnight, then she could do anything.

"Hey, Hannah," Ryan said as he opened the door to let her in. "Great costume."

"Thanks," Hannah replied, taking in Ryan's mad scientist lab coat, nerdy red bow tie, and geeky glasses. "Yours too."

"How is everything?" Ryan whispered as he led Hannah to the basement. "Is the ghost gone for good?"

Hannah grinned. "Definitely."

Hannah met Jake, the drummer, and then they rehearsed the song a few times. Finally, they put their instruments away and headed over to the snack table. The plan was to enjoy most of the party and then play their song toward the end.

Guests started to arrive, and Hannah was thrilled to see Paisley show up in her soccer uniform.

"Is that your costume?" Hannah asked.

Paisley grimaced. "I know it's lame, but I didn't have time to come up with anything else. Plus, I just came from my game."

"I think it's awesome," Hannah told her friend.

Paisley sighed. "I don't," she said. "I wish I had time to come up with something, but my schedule's been so busy I can barely think straight. And I definitely haven't had any time for my friends." She looked pointedly at Hannah. "I know I haven't been the best friend lately, and I'm really sorry. But I'm going to have more room in my schedule soon, I promise."

"That's great," Hannah said. "How come?"

"I decided to drop clarinet," Paisley replied. "Now that we're in seventh grade, I have a lot more schoolwork, and it's just been too much. I don't want to quit soccer, and I really like student council, so clarinet has to go."

"That's a bummer," Hannah said, thinking of how much it would stink to have to give up guitar. But then again, guitar was her only hobby, while Paisley had two others.

"Actually, I'm okay with it," Paisley said with a smile. "It means we'll be able to hang out more."

"That sounds great," Hannah agreed. "And I have a confession to make myself. I don't know if you've noticed, but I've been a little distracted lately."

She bit her lip. For some reason, this seemed like the right time to tell Paisley. Hannah felt braver about everything since she and Madison had confronted the ghost the previous night.

"Yeah, I noticed," Paisley said with a shrug. "I figured you were just missing Icky and adjusting to living with Madison and with your dad."

"That's true," Hannah agreed. "But it was a little more than just that." She took a deep breath. Then she told Paisley everything.

Paisley listened in shock, her mouth hanging open the entire time. "Why didn't you tell me any of this sooner?" she asked Hannah, incredulous. "I can't believe you were dealing with all of this on your own!"

"Well, I —" Hannah looked down, ashamed that she hadn't trusted her friend. "I thought maybe you wouldn't believe me. Remember that time when I lied to you about Ellie? When we made up, you said you didn't want to be friends with a liar. If you thought I was making up the stuff about the ghost, maybe you wouldn't want to be my friend anymore."

"Oh, Hannah!" Paisley exclaimed as she threw her arms around her friend. "We were *five*. That was a long time ago. And of course I would have believed you. You're my best friend."

Hannah hugged her back happily.

"I'm sorry I didn't tell you sooner," Hannah admitted. "From now on, whenever something's bothering me, you'll be the first to know."

"And vice versa!" Paisley said with a smile.

For the rest of the party, Hannah and Paisley danced and hung out with Taylor and some of Paisley's friends from the soccer team. Before Hannah knew it, Ryan came over to tell her they were going to perform soon.

"What's going on?" Paisley asked. "Who's performing?"

Hannah felt her cheeks flush. "Oh, that's one other thing I forgot to tell you," she squeaked. "I am. Wish me luck!"

Paisley's eyes widened in surprise, but Hannah didn't have time to explain. Instead, she just shrugged and followed Taylor and Ryan over to the makeshift stage. As she tuned her guitar, she glanced up to see Madison, Alexis, and Katie gaping at her.

Hannah was surprised to see them. She leaned over to Taylor.

"What are they doing here?" she asked, gesturing toward the three flappers. "I didn't realize you knew Madison."

Taylor rolled her eyes. "Ugh," she groaned. "Katie's our cousin, so my mom made us invite her. And she asked if she could bring her two friends because, of course, they don't go anywhere without each other."

Hannah glanced back at Madison and saw her give Hannah a small wave. It even looked like she mouthed the words "good luck," but Hannah couldn't be sure. She shook her head in disbelief as she stepped onto the stage.

Taylor stepped up to the microphone. "Hi, everyone," she told the crowd. "Thanks for coming to our party. We're The Headless Horsemen, and we're going to play our single for you. It's called 'Skeleton Riot.' Hope you like it, and happy Halloween!"

Taylor pounded out a few notes on the keyboard, and Jake and Ryan joined in. Hannah barely even had time for her nerves to set in, because suddenly her fingers were flying across the strings of her guitar.

"Watch out! Stand back! It's a skeleton riot," Taylor and Ryan sang. *"Watch out! Stand back! We're gonna get ya."*

It seemed like only seconds had passed before the song was over. Hannah couldn't believe it had gone by so quickly. Afterward, lots of the other kids at the party told her how great she had been.

Hannah felt someone tap her on the shoulder. She turned to see Madison standing there, flanked by Alexis on one side and Katie on the other. For a second, Hannah wasn't sure what she was going to say. Was she going to be mean and nasty like the old Madison? Or would she be the nicer version of Madison that Hannah had met for the first time the night before?

"Hey," Madison said. "I just wanted to tell you how great you were."

"Yeah," Alexis agreed. "That was awesome."

"Thanks," Hannah replied hesitantly, still not quite sure whether they were going to make fun of her or not.

"See you later," Madison said before the trio turned and headed toward the snack table.

Hannah sat down in a chair for a moment to take it all in. She couldn't believe everything that had happened in the last twenty-four hours. She had solved the mystery of the ghost cat, found Icky, somehow become not-quite-friends with her formerly evil stepsister, *and* overcome her stage fright. It was a lot to absorb.

As Hannah sipped a cup of warm apple cider, she thought of how much better things were now than they had been just a few weeks ago. Maybe living in Sleepy Hollow wasn't going to be so awful after all.

Suddenly, Hannah felt someone grab her free hand and pull her to her feet. She jumped up and found herself face-to-face with Ryan.

"Come on," he said eagerly. "This is my favorite song. Let's dance!"

Hannah grinned.

"Okay!" she replied.

Ryan and Hannah headed out onto the dance floor. Over her shoulder, Hannah saw Paisley dancing with Jake. She raised an eyebrow at Paisley, who just gave her an innocent shrug in return. Nearby, Madison, Katie, and Alexis were dancing. As weird as these first few weeks had been, it *was* going to be a great year. Hannah was sure of it.

BITE INTO THE NEXT POISON APPLE, IF YOU DARE!

On Saturday, I sleep in. The long weekend stretches out ahead of me. Back in New York, I know, Eve and Mallory will be shopping at Bloomingdale's, but for once, I don't feel like I'm missing out. There are plenty of things to do here in L.A., like seeing the Hollywood Walk of Fame, or, as Mom suggested last night, hitting up Rodeo Drive.

I'm about to go downstairs and remind Mom of these plans when the wail of sirens outside makes me jump. I realize then that I'd been hearing the sirens, distantly, all morning. But in my fog of drowsiness, I didn't pay attention.

I step out onto my balcony. It's an overcast, slightly chilly day. But the air still smells sweet, like flowers and oranges. Across the street, by the entrance to the beach, I see police cars, news vans, and a crowd of concerned-looking people.

A finger of worry pokes me. It could be a shark sighting, or maybe a skateboarder fell and skinned his knee. But a niggling feeling in my gut tells me it's something more sinister. Something that I'll find important.

I go over to my computer and type in *Santa Monica* and the word *attack*. A second later, a headline pops up and makes my jaw drop:

SURFER FOUND ON SANTA MONICA BEACH WITH SEVERE NECK WOUND; IN STABLE CONDITION AT HOSPITAL

"Oh my gosh," I whisper.

In what was believed to be a wild animal attack, a twenty-one-year-old surfer was bitten this morning. . . . The young man recalls "a dark, winged thing, like a bird, maybe" flying at him before he blacked out. . . .

He was found in an odd "frozen" state and suffered significant blood loss, but was able to communicate. . . . Police have no leads.

I shrink backward in my chair, terror gripping my throat. There's no way this is a coincidence. Somehow I feel responsible, as if I should have done something to prevent this. As if I need to do something now.

I glance wildly around my room. I could text Arabella, but it's unlikely she'd get back to me. I could call the police, but then I'd run the risk of everyone discovering *I* am a vampire. I could — I could — I close my eyes, overwhelmed. Then, in the next instant, there's nothing I *can* do.

Because I'm transforming into a bat.

POISON APPLE BOOKS

The Dead End

This Totally Bites!

Miss Fortune

Now You See Me...

Midnight Howl

Her Evil Twin

Curiosity Killed the Cat

At First Bite

THRILLING.
BONE-CHILLING.
THESE BOOKS
HAVE BITE!